"Look, I didn't mean to get out of line just now,"

Luke mumbled to Josie, whose lips were pink and kiss-swollen, her cheeks brighter than the weather alone explained. "I don't exactly know what happened. I guess I just got overly ex...ex..." *Oh, crimony, O'Dell—say anything except excited!* "...exuberant."

Overly exuberant—oh, that was a good one. Flyin' catfish—where the heck had he come up with that?

Josie's cheeks flamed.

Luke swallowed painfully and averted his eyes. "Anyway, I'm sorry. It won't happen again. We'd better get going. We've got a lot of ground to cover."

He stalked toward the pickup, wishing some of that ground would just open up and swallow him now.

Dear Reader,

This July, Silhouette Romance cordially invites you to a month of marriage stories, based upon *your* favorite themes. There's no need to RSVP; just pick up a book, start reading…and be swept away by romance.

The month kicks off with our Fabulous Fathers title, *And Baby Makes Six*, by talented author Pamela Dalton. Two single parents marry for convenience' sake, only to be surprised to learn they're expecting a baby of their own!

In Natalie Patrick's *Three Kids and a Cowboy*, a woman agrees to stay married to her husband just until he adopts three adorable orphans, but soon finds herself longing to make the arrangement permanent. And the romance continues when a beautiful wedding consultant asks her sexy neighbor to pose as her fiancé in *Just Say I Do* by RITA Award-winning author Lauryn Chandler.

The reasons for weddings keep coming, with a warmly humorous story of amnesia in Vivian Leiber's *The Bewildered Wife;* a new take on the runaway bride theme in *Have Honeymoon, Need Husband* by Robin Wells; and a green card wedding from debut author Elizabeth Harbison in *A Groom for Maggie*.

Here's to your reading enjoyment!

Melissa Senate
Senior Editor
Silhouette Romance

Please address questions and book requests to:
Silhouette Reader Service
U.S.: 3010 Walden Ave., P.O. Box 1325, Buffalo, NY 14269
Canadian: P.O. Box 609, Fort Erie, Ont. L2A 5X3

HAVE HONEYMOON, NEED HUSBAND

Robin Wells

Silhouette
ROMANCE™
Published by Silhouette Books
America's Publisher of Contemporary Romance

To Ken, who roped my heart.

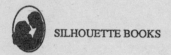 SILHOUETTE BOOKS

ISBN 0-373-19238-X

HAVE HONEYMOON, NEED HUSBAND

Printed in U.S.A.

Books by Robin Wells

Silhouette Romance

The Wedding Kiss #1185
Husband and Wife...Again #1214
Have Honeymoon, Need Husband #1238

ROBIN WELLS

Before becoming a full time writer, Robin was a public-relations executive whose career ran the gamut from writing and producing award-winning videos to organizing pie-throwing classes taught by circus clowns. At other times in her life she has been a model, a reporter and even a charm school teacher. But her lifelong dream was to become an author, a dream no doubt inspired by having parents who were both librarians and who passed on their love of books.

Robin lives just outside of New Orleans with her husband and two young daughters, Taylor and Arden. Although New Orleans is known as America's Most Romantic City, Robin says her personal romantic inspiration is her husband, Ken.

Robin is an active member of the Southern Louisiana chapter of the Romance Writers of America. She won the national association's 1995 Golden Heart Award for best short contemporary novel and was a finalist in the 1994 "Heart of the Rockies" RWA contest.

When she's not writing, Robin enjoys gardening, antiquing, discovering new restaurants and spending time with her family.

JOSIE'S TIPS
FOR A FABULOUS HONEYMOON

1) Leave your cheating groom at the altar–he was a louse anyway!

2) Go solo on your honeymoon–why waste the quaint dude ranch experience?

3) Get the hunky ranch owner to escort you on all of your honeymoon activities–especially the moonlit camping trip for two.

4) Get ready to walk down the aisle again–this time with the right groom.

Chapter One

The bridal veil sagged over Josie Randall's right eye again.

"Blasted thing," she muttered to herself, pulling a hand from the steering wheel long enough to toss it out of her face. She was having a hard enough time driving through the backwoods of northeastern Oklahoma in the pouring rain at night without having to play peekaboo with a ridiculous piece of netting at the same time. For the umpteenth time since she'd bolted from the church in Tulsa, she tugged at the headpiece, but it was pinned too firmly in her hair to remove with one hand.

She couldn't wait to get to the guest ranch and take the darned thing off—along with the wedding gown. The elaborate, pearl-encrusted dress was designed for standing at an altar, not sitting through a two-hour car trip. The waistband was about to pinch her in two, and the back of the dress bunched beneath her in a miserable lump.

Josie squirmed, trying to find a more comfortable position. "Now I know why they call it a train," she grumbled aloud. "My caboose feels like it's about to derail."

The sooner she got out of the torturous ensemble, the sooner she could put the whole horrible affair behind her and start getting on with her life. A life that from here on out, she thought resolutely, she would fully control herself.

Josie's mouth firmed with determination as she steered the car around a curve on the dark two-lane highway. She'd nearly made the worst mistake of her life, and it was all because she'd doubted her own judgment. She hadn't trusted her own feelings and intuition, and had nearly let her well-meaning but misguided family push her into marrying a man who'd turned out to be nothing but a two-timing, self-centered, greedy, loathsome *cad*.

The thought of Robert sent a fresh surge of outrage pulsing through her. Thank heavens she'd discovered his true colors before the ceremony! If she hadn't happened to wander down that back hallway of the church in an attempt to calm her nerves, she wouldn't have overheard him talking with the best man—and she wouldn't have learned the *real* reason he wanted to marry her.

Josie's fingers tightened on the steering wheel. How could she have been so blind? How could she have been so gullible? More importantly, how could she have thought for even one nanosecond that she loved him? If she had, surely she wouldn't be feeling this overwhelming sense of relief right now.

How, oh *how* could she have been so naive, so unaware, so foolish?

Thinking about it made her whole body tense and caused her foot to inadvertently press down on the accelerator. The car skidded on the wet pavement, jerking Josie's thoughts back to present.

If she wanted to arrive at the ranch in one piece, she

needed to focus all of her attention on her driving, she told herself. There'd be plenty of time later to sort things out. A whole week, in fact. Buying herself time to think was the main reason she'd decided to go ahead and come on the honeymoon—sans groom.

The rain was falling harder now, slashing across her windshield so fast that her wipers were virtually useless. Josie slowed the car and hunched forward, searching for the turnoff. According to the directions in the brochure, the dude ranch should be along here somewhere.

Her headlights picked up the gleam of a metal sign. Squinting, she leaned over the wheel and peered through the downpour. She couldn't read all the words in the split second of vision the wipers afforded, but she could make out the Lazy O brand at the top. With a sigh of relief, she turned onto the narrow dirt road that cut through the dense stand of oaks.

She hadn't traveled more than a few yards before she realized the rain had turned the road into a slick, muddy quagmire. Apprehension tightened around her chest like a giant vise. Oh, mercy. There was no place to turn around, and she didn't dare try to back out onto the highway. She had no choice but to keep going.

Clutching the steering wheel as if it might bound out of her grasp at any moment, she inched the car along, trying to avoid the obvious ruts. The downpour and the darkness made it impossible to see anything but a few scant feet in front of her headlights. The farther she went, the worse the road became. If she didn't get to the lodge soon, she was likely to find herself stuck for the night.

She rounded a curve in the road and saw a light shining ahead. "There it is," she muttered in relief. She couldn't make out anything about the building, but it looked as if it was just around the next bend.

Suddenly the rear end of her car swerved, then fishtailed. The next thing she knew, the vehicle was wedged in a deep, muddy rut, the back tires spinning uselessly.

Oh, terrific. The perfect ending to a perfect day.

She peered through the windshield, squinting to see through the rain. The light was straight ahead, probably no more than a hundred feet away. It was within easy walking distance, but with no umbrella or raincoat she'd ruin her delicate gown in a matter a seconds.

On the other hand, if she tried to wait out the storm, she might still be waiting come morning.

She glanced down at the elaborate gown. As far as she was concerned, it was ruined, anyway. Besides, the darn thing was so uncomfortable it felt like it was lined with razor blades.

"What the heck," she muttered, switching off the engine.

She was tired of playing it safe, tired of trying to avoid criticism, tired of caring so much about everyone else's opinion. Most of all, she was tired of not trusting her own judgment, tired of second-guessing her every decision.

With that thought in mind, Josie decisively yanked open the door, stepped out of the car—and promptly slid into the mud.

The rain pummeled her like a prize fighter, drenching her in a matter of seconds. She struggled to regain her footing, but the mud was so slick she flopped back down like a grounded fish. She finally managed to haul herself upright, only to trip on the hem of her gown and again plop in the mire, this time facedown.

The rain continued to pelt her. Panting, she pushed herself into a sitting position. That dratted veil was in her eyes again. She swiped at it with a muddy hand, smearing thick red clay all over it, only to have it immediately fall back in her face.

Dadblast the thing! She'd deal with it once she made it indoors. Right now she needed to concentrate all her energy on the simple task of standing up. The wet gown weighed as much as a small elephant.

Kicking off her shoes, she hoisted the heavy skirt in her arms and struggled to her feet. Mud squished through her sheer stockings and oozed between her toes as she lurched blindly down the road, heading toward the light. Mercy, she hoped it hung over the lodge door!

The muddy veil obscured her vision, but her hand made contact with a doorknob. Relief surged through her as she tugged the door open, staggered inside and slammed it shut behind her.

"What the hell..." a deep male voice roared.

It smelled like a barn. Confused, Josie dropped her dripping skirts and pushed back the mud-soaked veil.

Oh, heavens. It *was* a barn!

A loud snort jerked Josie's attention to her right, and the source of the noise made her freeze. An enormous, wild-eyed horse reared, whinnied and charged directly at her.

Helpless to move, she watched in horror as a tall, dark-haired man lunged at the beast and grabbed the harness. The animal reared on its hind legs and pawed the air, nostrils flaring, teeth bared. A flash of hooves sailed past her face, missing her by mere inches.

In terror, Josie watched the beast turn and buck. The man jumped aside, narrowly dodging disaster as the powerful back hooves struck the very spot he'd stood just a second before.

"Easy, boy. Easy." The man spoke softly, but his grip on the horse was strong and sure. His biceps bulged under his plaid flannel shirt as he grasped the halter under the animal's chin, backed the beast into a stall and slammed the gate closed with a loud bang.

The sound reverberated in the air. Jessie leaned her head against the wall and let out a long, ragged breath. Her chest hurt, and she realized she'd been holding her breath.

The man strode toward her, his dark eyes glaring, his broad shoulders squared. "What the hell do you think you're doing? You nearly got yourself killed!"

His build was as powerful as the horse's, and from the look in his eyes, he might be just as dangerous. Josie tried to take a step backward, but her back was already against the wall. "I—I'm sorry. I thought this was the Lazy O Lodge."

The scowl on his tanned face deepened. "If you can't tell a barn from a lodge, then maybe you'd just better go back to the city where you belong. The number-one rule around here is no visitors allowed on the working parts of the ranch without an escort." He raked her from head to toe with a scathing gaze. "What in blue blazes are you doing in a getup like that, anyway? Halloween's not for another two weeks."

Josie glanced down at her wet, mud-smeared gown. She knew she must look like an escapee from a sideshow exhibit, but she'd be darned if she'd offer the man an explanation. He was too rude to warrant one.

Doing her best to disguise her rattled nerves, Josie raised her chin. "I said I was sorry," she said stiffly. "If you'll just give me directions to the lodge, I'll get out of your way."

"How'd you get here, anyway?"

"I drove in from the highway. I was following the directions in the brochure."

The man gave a disgusted shake of his head that sent an

unruly lock of hair cascading over his forehead. "No, you weren't."

Josie bristled. She'd had a horrible day, and she was in no mood to take any guff from a disagreeable ranch hand. "I most certainly was. The directions said to turn at the sign, and that's exactly what I did," she said frostily.

"You turned at the sign that says Lazy O Lodge Ahead. If you'd driven on five hundred feet, you would have seen a larger sign with an arrow."

Josie felt a familiar cringing sensation—the one she always felt when she'd just made a mistake. *Oh, no, you don't*, she told herself fiercely. *You're not going to let this man make you feel like your judgment is faulty just because you couldn't read the entire sign in the pouring rain.*

Who did he think he was, anyway, talking to her like that? She wasn't going to stand for it. "Do you work at the Lazy O?"

The man's lip curved upward. "You might say that."

Josie stretched her frame to its full five-foot-four height and took a step forward, striving for her most imposing demeanor. "Well, then, sir, I'll make you a deal. If you'll spare me any more pearls of wisdom and simply tell me how to get to the lodge, I'll refrain from mentioning your insufferably rude behavior to Mr. O'Dell."

"Oh, you will, will you?" The man's mouth widened into a smile, a smile as infuriating as it was devastating. The expression transformed his face, bringing the hard, masculine planes and angles into a shockingly attractive alignment.

For some reason, the sight knocked Josie off her stride. She compensated for her shaken composure by directing the full force of her fury at him—a fury that had been building inside her ever since she'd learned the truth about her would-be groom.

Her hands balled into fists at her sides. "On second thought, I won't. I used to work in a hotel, and I thought I'd seen everything, but I've never heard of anyone in the hospitality industry treating a guest trying to check in as rudely as you've just treated me. I'm sure Mr. O'Dell will be interested to learn of your behavior."

To her chagrin, he appeared amused. "I'm afraid you're out of luck, miss. For starters, we don't have any rooms available. We're booked solid."

"But I have reservations."

The man's eyes narrowed skeptically. "All of our guests have already checked in, except for the honeymoon couple."

He suddenly froze and stared, his gaze traveling from her mud-covered stockings to her clay-encrusted veil. His eyebrows flew up like the wings of a crow. "Holy molasses! Is that a wedding gown you're wearing?"

Josie took a perverse pleasure in his dumbfounded expression. "It is," she said with all the dignity she could muster. "And if you'd point me in the direction of the honeymoon cabin, I'd like to change out of it as soon as possible. My car got stuck on the road and I fell in the mud."

The man stared at her. "You're Mrs. Olsen?"

"No. I'm Josie Randall."

He ran a hand through his thick, dark hair, his expression confused. "But the reservation is for the Olsens."

"Yes. But it's on my credit card, and my credit card says Josie Randall."

The man studied her for a moment, apparently processing the information. He shook his head. "I've never understood why a woman would marry a man and refuse to take his name, but that's your business. So where's your husband?"

"I don't have one."

His dark brows pulled together. "But you just said you'd reserved the honeymoon cabin."

"I did."

"And you don't have a husband?" His expression clearly said he was having doubts about her sanity.

"We didn't— I mean, the wedding didn't—" Josie's throat swelled with emotion, and to her horror, she realized she was about to cry.

Oh, no! She always cried when she was upset—ever since she'd been a young child. It was nothing more than an emotional release valve, but this man was sure to take it as a sign of weakness. The last thing she wanted to do was break down in front of him.

She drew a deep breath and tried to forestall the inevitable. "The w-wedding was c-c-called off," she finally managed to say in a tear-choked voice.

She ducked her head, and the mud-streaked veil sagged forward. She gratefully took refuge behind it. Her pride had taken enough of a blow today without the additional embarrassment of having this impossible man see her cry.

"Oh, hey... I'm sorry." His deep voice was contrite. "That must be rough. I had no idea..."

The veil abruptly lifted. The man stood in front of her, his dark eyes worried and apologetic.

"Here." He pulled a handkerchief out of his pocket and dabbed at her face, first drying her cheeks, then gently wiping her forehead. "You have some mud here, too," he said, rubbing the cloth across her chin.

His gentleness jarred Josie as much as his earlier rudeness. She stared up at him, surprised to find his face so close, his eyes so dark and concerned.

Still holding the hanky, he placed his hands on her shoulders. His fingers were warm on the wet silk. "Look, I'm really sorry. I didn't realize..."

His change of demeanor disoriented her. Or maybe it was his nearness. She was keenly aware of the weight of his hands, of his masculine scent, of his breath on her face.

Her gaze fastened on his lips, and a wild, alien thought formed in her mind: what would it feel like to kiss him?

Merciful heavens, where had that thought come from? She lowered her gaze, suddenly self-conscious. Don't be ridiculous, she told herself; it's not like the thought is tattooed on your forehead. He's a cowboy, not a mind reader.

"I've never had a guest show up in a wedding gown before," he said apologetically. He gently tilted up her chin. The pads of his fingers were callused, and the rasp of them on her skin made her heart rate soar.

Funny…she couldn't remember a man ever touching her face before. Certainly not Robert. And she'd never known fingers could be so warm. Why, his seemed to warm her straight to the bone.

"With all the mud, I thought you were wearing some sort of costume—Swamp Girl or Creature from the Black Lagoon or something. It's close to Halloween and I've had some guests do some pretty weird things…." His brow knit in concern as he looked down at her. "Are you okay?"

Josie nodded, not yet trusting herself to speak. He smelled like leather and horseflesh and hard work, with a subtle undernote of soap. The scent was rich and male—far more appealing than all of Robert's expensive colognes and grooming products, she thought distractedly. Her gaze again fell to his lips.

"I'm sorry I yelled at you. I was upset because you nearly got yourself killed," he explained. "That stallion's got a mean streak a mile wide. In fact, I'm trying to sell him for just that reason. A potential buyer is coming to look at him in the morning, so I was grooming him when you walked in." His hand moved back to her shoulder. His eyes were kind and worried. "I go ballistic when guests put themselves in danger. Sorry I overreacted, Josie."

The frank, open apology took her by surprise. There weren't many men who would own up to a mistake so readily, she thought.

But it was the way he'd said her name that really jolted her. His deep rumble of a voice had wrapped around it like a velvet cloak, making it sound appealing and feminine and...sensuous.

What the heck was the matter with her? Her pulse was racing and skittering, and her thoughts were flying off in all kinds of dangerous and inappropriate directions. She must have taken leave of her senses, responding this way to some man she'd just met.

She must be more overwrought than she'd realized. Maybe she was even suffering some type of post-traumatic syndrome. After all, it *had* been a nerve-wracking day This behavior was so far out of character she could barely recognize it as her own.

Josie folded her arms protectively across her chest. "Let's just forget about it," she said. "If you'll help me get to the lodge, I won't mention anything to Mr. O'Dell."

The man dropped his hands from her shoulders, but the heat from his touch remained. He gave a lopsided grin. "Too late."

Was he deliberately keeping her off balance? "What do you mean?"

Folding one arm across his flat stomach and the other behind his back, he made a courtly bow. "Luke O'Dell at your service, ma'am."

"But the man in the brochure photos—"

"Was my father. He died six months ago."

"Oh!" Josie murmured. "I'm so sorry."

"Me, too." A flicker of pain crossed his face. He diverted his gaze to the toes of his cowboy boots, then shoved his hands into the pockets of his well-worn jeans. "Look, Josie, I know guests are told payment is nonrefundable without a week's notice, but under the circumstances I'll be happy to give you your money back."

"Oh, I don't want my money back. After all I've been through, I really need a week's vacation."

Luke gazed at the mud-stained creature before him and tried to suppress his dismay. The last thing he needed right now was a half-crazy, lovelorn woman moping around the ranch. She'd probably require extra attention, and the lodge staff was overextended as it was.

He shook his head dubiously. "It would probably be better if you come back some other time. All of our guests this week are couples, and I don't want you to spend the week feeling like a third wheel."

"But I won't be participating in the group activities. I'm registered for the honeymoon package."

She wasn't half-crazy; she was full-blown loco! Luke stared at her incredulously. "You want to do the honeymoon package activities *alone?*"

"That's right."

"You want to go on a moonlight trail ride, a private cookout, an overnight canoe trip...*by yourself?*"

Her chin moved ever so slightly upward. When she spoke, her voice had a defensive edge. "That's right."

Oh, boy. What was she—some kind of emotional masochist? It sounded like she'd come here to wallow in her misery. If so, she'd no doubt make the whole ranch miserable in the bargain.

He rubbed his jaw, trying to think of a way to dissuade her, then glanced down and realized a huge puddle was forming beneath her on the barn floor. She was soaking wet and probably freezing; there was no point in trying to reason with her while she was in this condition. He had no choice but to put her up for the night. Hopefully she'd change her mind tomorrow.

Luke pulled his hands out of his pockets and straightened. "Look, I'll tell you what—you can sleep on it and we'll see how you feel about things in the morning. The refund offer will still stand. In the meantime, I'm sure you're anxious to get out of your wet clothes."

She nodded, and the motion made the veil flop in her face again. He reached out and pushed it back, arranging the whole thing behind her shoulders.

"I'll take you to your cabin. My pickup is just outside." He motioned toward the door.

She turned in the direction he indicated, but the bottom of her dress didn't turn with her. She stooped to unwind it from around her ankles and stumbled.

Luke's hand shot out and caught her around the waist. He felt as though he'd just grabbed ahold of a live electrical wire. Her skin felt warm and supple and sexy as sin beneath the thin, wet fabric, and touching it sent shock waves pulsing up his arm.

Attraction, strong and unexpected, surged through him. He hadn't felt anything this good in a long, long time. He swallowed hard. "Do you need some help with that thing?" he asked.

She looked up and nodded, and his fingers tightened involuntarily around her waist. Touching her like this made him notice things about her that had previously escaped his attention. How could he have failed to notice before now that her eyes were the exact color of a field of bluebonnets, or that she had an adorable upturned nose dusted with a faint sprinkling of freckles?

Giving himself a mental shake, he cleared his throat and tried to clear his mind. "What can I do?"

"Could you please lift up my skirt?"

The request conjured up an image that made Luke break into a sweat. His eyes skimmed over her, overlooking the mud and noting instead how the wet silk clung to her curves, outlining her high, round breasts and narrow waist. Holy mackerel; how could he have missed all this before now? That veil had been hiding more than he'd realized.

He couldn't repress a wolfish grin. "Well, now...there's a request I don't hear every day."

He liked the way she blushed, and he loved the way her smile lit up her face like a switched-on lightbulb. It had the same effect on him, making him feel unaccountably turned on.

"This thing must weigh a ton," she explained, plucking at her sodden skirt. "And it's wound so tightly around my feet I can't bend down without falling over."

Reluctantly he relinquished his hold on her and untangled the dress. "It's heavy, all right." He draped the train over the arm she held out to him. "I've got full-grown heifers that weigh less."

Her laugh was soft and warm. A dimple flashed in her right cheek, and he found himself searching for another witty remark so he could see it again.

He'd be better off searching for a way to get her off the ranch, he warned himself. The lodge manager had walked off the job last month, and he had his hands full trying to run both the ranch and the lodge at the same time. The last thing he needed right now was an added distraction.

Especially a distraction exhibiting as many red flags as Josie. For starters, she was sure to be an emotional mess. He'd vowed he'd never get involved with another woman recovering from a recently broken romance, and it didn't get any more recent than this. Tonight was supposed to be her wedding night, for Pete's sake.

Besides, he had no intention of falling for a city slicker again. Next time around he was determined to find a good, solid, practical woman who'd been born and bred in the country and knew exactly what ranch life was like.

He was out of his mind to even be noticing things like the way her top lip had two luscious peaks that exactly mimicked the curves on her chest, and…

He abruptly realized he was staring. With an effort he forced his eyes away. He needed to stop thinking about her. She was clearly off-limits.

But the fact did nothing to stop another rush of electricity from charging through him when he took her arm. "I'll help you to the truck, since you seem to have a hard time getting around in that thing."

Her heart-shaped face grew worried. "I'll get mud all over your seat."

It was a practical consideration, and he was grateful she'd thought of it. He'd been too preoccupied gawking at her to think of it himself. "I have a tarp in the back. Wait here and I'll throw it over the upholstery, then I'll come back and get you."

"I'll need my luggage. It's in the back seat of my car."

He hadn't thought of that, either. It was as if his mind had taken a vacation south. South of his belt buckle, that was. "I'll get you settled in the truck, then I'll go get it."

He rapidly ducked outdoors, grateful for the excuse to get some fresh air and clear his head.

The rain had slowed to a drizzle. Too bad, he thought as he sloshed through the soggy leaves on the way to his pickup.

Because he sure could have used a cold shower.

Chapter Two

"How did you hear about the Lazy O?" Luke asked as he steered the pickup along the narrow gravel road that led from the barn to the lodge.

"My travel agent gave me a brochure," Josie replied, gripping the seat as the truck bounced over the rough terrain. "Everything sounds wonderful!"

That was the problem with that blasted brochure, Luke thought glumly; his father had gone overboard on the descriptions, painting everything in glowing terms and flowery, romantic language.

Especially the honeymoon cabin, Luke thought as he braked the pickup to a jerky stop in front of it. He'd bet his best bull she'd be disappointed to discover it was nothing more than a ramshackle old log cabin fronted by a long, covered porch.

"Here we are," Luke said, glancing over at Josie and bracing himself for a string of complaints.

She peered through the truck's rain-streaked window. "Oh, it's beautiful!" She looked up and flashed that dimple at him before turning back to the view. "So rustic and secluded. Just like the brochure describes."

Stifling his surprise, Luke followed her gaze. He'd always thought the cabin was great, too, but it wasn't everyone's reaction. Nestled amid a backdrop of oaks and pines and illuminated by a lantern-shaped light shining on the porch, it looked like it belonged in another century.

"My father built it years ago as a guest house," Luke explained. "He designed it after a cabin in the Rockies where he honeymooned with my mother. The main lodge is behind it, just past those trees."

"You wouldn't know there was anything around for miles."

"In the good old days, there wasn't."

Josie couldn't miss the tension in his voice. "You sound like you don't much like the lodge."

Luke's shoulders tightened. How had they gotten off on this topic, anyway? He shrugged in a show of casualness. "I'm a rancher, not an innkeeper. Turning the Lazy O into a dude ranch was my father's idea."

He switched off the engine and reached for the door handle, wanting to forestall any more questions. "Stay put. I'll come around and help you down so you don't get tangled up in that dress again."

She took his hands and stepped down, lurching against him as her feet hit the ground. He inhaled sharply at the contact of her soft breasts against his chest and caught a heady whiff of her scent—something soft and subtle, like baby powder and fresh flowers, mingled with a deep, earthy aroma that seemed somehow familiar.

Mud—that was what smelled familiar. And she was probably smearing it all over him. Boy, was he ever a sorry sack of hormones, getting all muddle headed and romantic over the scent of mud!

Scrunching his forehead into a frown, he pulled away.

The sudden motion made her lurch again. "Sorry," she murmured. "This darn gown..."

Without thinking, he bent and swooped her up, one arm under her knees, the other around her back.

Her arm involuntarily flew around his neck. Her face was inches from his, her eyes wide with alarm. "What are you doing?"

Good question. He was as shocked to find her in his arms as she was to be there.

There was that scent again. Jiminy—he didn't care if it was partly mud, it still smelled downright delicious. She felt that way, too. Even in her sodden gown she was no heavier than a newborn colt, but the wet silk made her as slippery as a greased pig.

He bounced her slightly in the air as he adjusted his grip, searching his mind for a way to explain his purely reflexive action. "That blasted dress is a hazard," he muttered. "My insurance company would cancel my liability coverage if they knew we had guests running around outfitted like that."

Carrying her as easily as he'd tote a bale of hay, he strode rapidly to the covered porch and set her down outside the door. No way was he going to carry her across the threshold; he was having a hard enough time keeping his thoughts about her under control without acting like a surrogate bridegroom.

The imprint of her warm, wet body burned against him long after he released her, and he had a physical reaction to it. Jeezem Pete, he responded like a teenage boy every time he touched her.

So stop touching her, O'Dell, he chided himself sarcastically.

He fumbled in his pocket for a master key, then unlocked

the door. It swung open. He reached in and flipped on a light. "Here you are. I'll get your bags."

She was still standing on the porch when he returned from the truck. He plopped the bags down by the door and eyed her warily. "You ought to get out of those wet clothes and into a hot shower before you catch pneumonia." The last thing he wanted was to have her laid up convalescing, needing to be waited on hand and foot.

"I don't want to track mud inside. I think I should take off the dress out here."

The thought did strange things to his pulse rate. He cleared his throat and turned to go. "I'll give you some privacy."

"Wait!"

Now what? He swiveled around.

"I...I can't undo the buttons myself."

She turned and pointed over her shoulder. A long row of tiny buttons ran from the neck of the gown to below her waist—dozens of buttons, each about the size of a raisin, each fastened with tiny loops of thread.

"Oh, for heaven's sake..."

"I'm sorry to be such a bother." Her voice had a suspicious warble in it.

Oh, criminy; she wasn't going to cry again, was she?

"I realize it's beyond the call of duty, but I'm freezing, and..."

"I'll call the housekeeper to help you."

He strode into the cabin, picked up the phone and punched out Consuela's number. No answer. No answer in the lodge kitchen, either.

Great, just great. He'd have to deal with this himself.

The screen door banged behind him as he rejoined Josie on the porch. "Turn around and stand still." The words came out more harshly than he'd intended.

She presented her slender back to him. He stepped forward, pushed her veil out of the way and tackled the top button. It sat at the nape of her neck, covered by damp tendrils of shoulder-length dark hair. He brushed the wet strands aside, his fingers feeling huge and awkward, and tried to ignore the rush of arousal that tightened his body.

The woman was wreaking havoc with his libido. Maybe it was because this was supposed to be her wedding night—a night when her skin was supposed to be touched, her lips were meant to be tasted, those enticing curves were to be explored and caressed....

By another man, O'Dell. For heaven's sake, get a grip.

His fingers fumbled, and the button tore off in his hands. "Sorry," he muttered, moving on to the next one.

It had evidently been too long since he'd been around a woman. He hadn't dated much since his divorce, and that had been five years ago. Judging from the way he was reacting now, it was time he got back in the saddle and started socializing again.

The button popped free. His fingers edged down to attack the next one. Josie shifted and sighed, and he struggled to rein in his thoughts.

This wasn't the time to be thinking about dating, he reminded himself. Ever since he'd come back to the ranch, he'd had his hands full, trying to take care of everything his father had neglected when he'd opened that damn lodge. And without a lodge manager, he had that to worry about, too. He had a full plate in front of him without taking on something as time-consuming as trying to meet and get to know a woman.

Besides, he hated all the things dating involved—getting dressed up, making small talk, trying to figure out what was real and what was pretense, trying to keep from getting dragged down a wedding aisle.

Standing in front of him was a perfect example of what he most wanted to avoid and what was often so hard to detect—a marriage-minded woman with a lot of emotional baggage, still carrying a torch for another guy. At least with this one he knew what he was dealing with.

Another button came off in his hand. "I'm afraid I'm pulling off as many buttons as I'm unfastening," he told her.

"That's okay." Her voice was muffled by the veil. "The dress is a loss, anyway. If it's easier, you can just yank them all off."

The thought of ripping off her dress had undeniable appeal—so much so that he deliberately resisted the urge, furrowing his brow in concentration and meticulously undoing the buttons one at a time.

"There," he muttered when he'd finally unfastened the last one.

The fabric gapped to reveal something lacy and sheer underneath the dress. His imagination running wild, he swallowed hard and stepped back as she turned around.

She was shivering, he realized with a start. He'd attributed the trembling he'd felt as he'd unbuttoned her dress to his own shaking hands. "You need to get inside," he told her. "Do you want me to carry in your bags?"

She rubbed her arms, her teeth chattering. "What I really want is to get thawed out as soon as possible. Would you turn around for a moment?"

Luke complied. Fabric rustled, the cabin door creaked and soft footsteps thudded on the wooden floor.

"You can turn around now," she called from inside the cabin.

Her dress lay in a heap on the porch...along with two muddy, crumpled stockings. A trail of muddy footprints led inside the cabin to the closed bathroom door. He heard a rush of water from the shower.

Luke exhaled harshly and eyed the stockings again, wondering how she'd held them up. His tantalizing conjectures about her undergarments were cut short when his gaze fell again on the crumpled wedding gown.

It was a pitiful sight, all that lace and silk puddled in a muddy mess on the porch, and it sent a wave of sympathy surging through him. What had once been a beautiful dress was rumpled and ruined, and her dreams were no doubt in the same condition. What was supposed to have been the happiest day of her life had ended in heartbreak.

He wondered why the wedding had been canceled. Had she called it off, or had the groom? Obviously someone had—and at the very last minute, judging from the way she was dressed.

One thing was for certain: she was sure to be feeling awful. He should have been looking for ways to comfort her instead of leering at her like a cowboy Casanova.

A stab of guilt shot through him. No matter how much he disliked it, as long as the Lazy O was operated as a guest ranch, he had an obligation to care for his guests in a manner worthy of the O'Dell name.

The least he could do was take her luggage inside. And while he was at it, he might as well start a fire in the fireplace, too.

Wrapped in a large white towel, with another wound turban-style around her hair, Josie opened the bathroom door fifteen minutes later to find Luke squatting before the fireplace, laying logs on a blaze of kindling.

The tight ache in her chest loosened a little at the sight of him. She was glad he was still there; the idea of solitude had begun to lose its appeal. In fact, as she'd stood under the shower and castigated herself for ever getting involved with Robert in the first place, she'd dreaded spending the evening alone with her thoughts.

How could she have allowed herself to be pushed and persuaded into nearly marrying a man she apparently didn't even know? All of the anger that had propelled her into action was fizzling into painfully familiar self-doubt.

Luke glanced up at her. She saw his Adam's apple bob before he abruptly turned away and picked up another piece of wood. "I thought you might like a fire," he said gruffly.

"Thanks." Her face burning, Josie wrapped the towel more tightly above her breasts and angled her body against the door so that only her head poked out. The towel covered more of her than some of her summer dresses did, but she was acutely aware of the fact she wore nothing under it. Something in the way his gaze swept over her told her he was aware of it, too.

She saw her suitcases near the door, but didn't want to parade across the room to get them. Her fingers tightened on the terry cloth. "Would you mind handing me the blue suitcase? I'll throw on some clothes and be right out."

Luke complied, and Josie ducked behind the door to rapidly pull on a sweatshirt, jeans and a pair of thick socks. Still toweling her damp hair, she stepped back into the living room.

The fire crackled and hissed, throwing a delicious warmth into the room. She walked up to it and gave a contented sigh. "This feels wonderful. Thanks."

Luke jammed his hands in his pockets. "No problem. I brought in some extra firewood for you. When you turn in for the night, just be sure the screen is in place."

"I will. Thanks."

"There's a path to the lodge on the right side of the cabin. Breakfast is served from seven until ten in the lodge dining room. There's a map of the ranch and some other information beside the phone.''

"Great.''

Luke watched her sling the towel over a chair and stretch out her hands to the fire. Man, she was pretty. Her hair fell in damp ringlets to her shoulders. Without the veil, he could see that it was the dark, rich color of a chocolate velvet cake.

He needed to get out of here. The sight of her in that towel had just about done him in. "Well, if you've got everything you need, I'll—''

A knock sounded at the door, interrupting his words. He strode across the room and opened it.

"Consuela.'' He pushed the door wider and stepped back, making room for a large, smiling woman who bustled in with an enormous tray.

"Manuel saw the lights on and told me our honeymoon couple had arrived,'' the woman announced in a lilting Spanish accent. "So I brought the candlelight dinner over.'' She gave Josie a sly grin as she set the huge tray on the pine plank dining table, then extended a plump hand. "Hello. I'm Consuela Perez.''

Josie shook Consuela's hand. "I'm Josie Randall.''

The older woman looked around the room. "Where's the lucky bridegroom?''

"I don't—'' Josie faltered for words. Silence hung awkwardly in the room.

Luke stepped forward. "Miss Randall's wedding was canceled. She's here alone.''

"Oh!'' Consuela's hands flew up, her face wrinkling with concern. "Oh, ¡Pobrecita! You poor darling. Is there anything I can do to help?''

Josie gave a self-conscious smile. "Thank you, but no.''

"Do you want to talk? I've got a good shoulder to cry on."

"I'm fine."

"It always helps to talk these things out. We can stay here, or you can come home with me—"

"That's very sweet of you, but I'm fine."

Consuela searched her face, her brown eyes large with concern. "Are you sure?"

"I'm sure."

"It's not good to be alone at a time like this," Consuela worried.

Luke watched the exchange, knowing Consuela would persist until Josie gave in or he baled her out. Consuela had the biggest heart in the world, but she was no respecter of privacy, and she was about as subtle as a gale-force wind. Her warm, mothering nature wouldn't allow her to take no for an answer if she was convinced someone needed nurturing.

He decided to try to change the subject. "Consuela is the lodge's head cook and housekeeper, Josie. She's the person who keeps the place running. We couldn't make it without her."

Josie smiled at her. "I'm sure that's true. I used to work in a hotel, and I know how important both positions are. It's a pleasure to meet you, Consuela."

Consuela preened, her stubby fingers smoothing her neat coil of gray-streaked black hair. "The pleasure is mine." She motioned toward the tray. "Look—I've brought you a nice dinner."

"I'm afraid I don't have much appetite," Josie admitted.

Consuela clucked like a worried hen. "But you must eat! The worst thing for a broken heart is an empty stomach, too."

Josie managed a smile. "All right...I'll try. Thank you."

"How about you?" Consuela turned to Luke. "You haven't eaten, either."

"I'll grab something later at the house."

Consuela rolled her eyes. "A can of cold spaghetti is not a meal." She glanced at Josie. "He lives alone and doesn't take care of himself. His animals eat better than he does."

"Why don't you join me?" Josie offered. "After all, it's a dinner for two. It's a shame for it to go to waste."

Consuela nodded approvingly. "That's a wonderful idea! Then neither of you will eat alone."

Luke suppressed a groan as Consuela bustled around, uncovering fragrant dishes and setting the table with the ranch's best china. He knew the housekeeper had set him up, but he couldn't think of a decent excuse to get out of it.

Consuela leaned her hefty frame across the table and lit a candle. "There!" she proclaimed, clasping her hands over her ample bosom. "All set."

She pulled out a chair and motioned to Josie, then handed Luke a bottle of champagne. "You can open this."

Luke looked hesitantly at Josie. "Under the circumstances, Consuela, I don't think—"

"I'd love some champagne," Josie said decisively.

Consuela nodded approvingly. "Wine is good for a broken heart."

"My heart isn't exactly broken—"

The large woman patted Josie's back consolingly. "There, there, dear. You don't have to explain. But you come and find Consuela if you want to chew the cat, okay?"

Josie blinked. "Pardon me?"

"She means chew the fat." Luke grinned.

Consuela shrugged. "Cat—fat—it makes no sense either way. But you come to me if you want to talk, okay?"

"Okay. Thank you."

"Enjoy. ¡*Buenos Noches!*" The large woman let herself out the door with a wave of her hand.

The room seemed suddenly very still and quiet. Luke awkwardly settled his large frame in the chair across from Josie.

"It all looks delicious," she remarked, surveying the spread of Caesar salad, prime beef, scalloped potatoes and baby carrots.

"Consuela's a wonderful cook. She and her husband have been with my family for over twenty-five years." Luke gave a wry grin. "She takes a lot of liberties with the English language—and with poking her nose in other people's business."

"She seems very kind."

Luke inclined his head. "She is. My mother died when I was twelve, and she practically raised me afterward." He set the bottle of champagne on the table. "She's right about being a good listener. If you get lonely and want to talk, you should take her up on her offer." He regarded Josie in the flickering candlelight. Her profile was delicate, almost fragile. Looking at it, he felt another stab of guilt at the way he'd exploded at her in the barn. It couldn't hurt for him to take a hint from Consuela and show a little sympathy. "For that matter, I can be a pretty good listener, too."

Josie reached for her napkin. "I'm okay. I'm actually relieved the wedding was called off."

Yeah, right. And he was going to sprout wings and fly. He'd seen denial before; in fact, he'd been in it himself. It was the first stage of the grieving process, and it was obviously where she was right now.

"I'm not heartbroken. I don't even really feel hurt." She

placed the napkin her on her lap. "I'm angry...mostly at myself. How could I have been so blind?"

He lifted a shoulder. "Well, you know what they say about love."

Josie leaned across the table, her face earnest. "That's just it. I didn't love him."

Boy, she must really be hurting if she needed to lie to herself like this. Well, he wasn't going to burst her bubble. Let her think whatever she wanted—whatever it took to get her through the night.

The thought made him reach for the champagne. "I'm sure everything will work out for the best." He popped the cork and sent it flying across the room, narrowly missing the fireplace, then sloshed some into Josie's glass. He filled his own and raised it in a toast. "To new beginnings."

Josie clinked her glass against his. "To a wonderful week at your ranch."

Luke frowned at her over the rim. Baby-sitting her tonight was one thing; doing it for a whole week was quite another. "Let's wait and see how you feel about things tomorrow."

"I already know how I'll feel...exactly the same." She took a sip of champagne. "I've wanted to visit a guest ranch all my life, and I'm not going to be cheated out of the experience just because Robert turned out to be a heel."

Luke's eyebrows rose in surprise. "You're the one who selected the Lazy O as a honeymoon destination?"

"Yes."

"That's a first."

Josie's brow knit in confusion. "What do you mean?"

Luke stabbed a bite of salad. "Most of the brides we see are dragged here kicking and screaming by a new husband who's watched one too many Westerns. After a couple of days, even the ones who initially think it sounded like fun are asking directions to the nearest mall.''

Josie daintily buttered a roll. ''I've always thought a ranch was the most romantic place on earth.''

Luke's lip curved into a grin. ''You've obviously never mucked out a stall.''

Josie laughed. ''Actually, I have. I spent my summers at a camp that offered riding lessons, and I made a habit of hanging around afterward to help out in the stables. It was a way to get to spend more time around the horses.''

Luke hid his surprise by spearing another leaf of romaine lettuce. Well, anything could be fun for a while, he thought—until the novelty wore off. His ex-wife had had the same reaction to life on the ranch.

He decided to change the subject. ''You mentioned you had hotel experience. Do you work at a hotel in Tulsa?''

Her blue eyes darkened like troubled water. ''No. I've been working as the office manager in my father's law firm for the past six months. But before that, I worked at the Royal Regent Hotel in Chicago.''

''I've heard of it. What did you do there?''

''A little of everything. I went through an eighteen-month management-training program, which meant I spent a few months in every department. Then I worked in convention sales for a year and half.''

''Why did you leave?''

Josie swirled the champagne in her glass. ''I didn't like the ethics of the new sales director. He didn't care about the clients, only about their money. He wanted me to promise things I knew the hotel couldn't deliver in order to get convention bookings, and I refused to lie. The hotel lost a major piece of business because I wouldn't do things his way. So I resigned before I got fired.''

Grudging admiration filled Luke's chest. As much as he

didn't want to like this woman, he couldn't help but respect her for refusing to compromise her principles. He raised his glass in a brief salute. "Good for you. Not many people have the courage of their convictions."

Josie gave a rueful grin. "I'm afraid my convictions didn't result in a very flattering job reference. I can't land another job in the hotel industry to save my life. So when my father asked me to fill in for a few months while his office manager recovered from major surgery, I moved back to Tulsa."

"Is that when you met your fiancé?"

Josie nodded. "He's an attorney at my father's firm. We started dating when I moved back, and three months later we were engaged."

Luke watched her toy with her salad, trying not to notice the way the candlelight gleamed on her dark hair and lit her blue eyes. Curiosity was burning a hole in him.

It was none of his business, he warned himself. The less he knew, the better off he'd be.

But he couldn't resist asking the question, anyway. "So what happened?"

"With the wedding? I narrowly avoided making the mistake of my life, that's what happened." She took a sip of champagne and regarded him over the rim of her glass. "Do you want the whole story?"

He was dying for it, but he feigned indifference. "Only if you want to tell me."

Josie put down her glass and leaned forward. "Well, I was a nervous wreck before the ceremony. I thought some exercise might calm my nerves, so I went for a walk down a back hallway of the church. I ended up outside the room where Robert and the best man were waiting. I could hear their voices through the air vents."

"And?" Luke prompted.

Josie's full lips thinned into a narrow line. "I learned a few things about the man I was about to marry."

"What things?"

"For starters, that his idea of matrimony doesn't include fidelity."

The whole thing was probably nothing more than a misunderstanding, Luke thought. Most likely the lovebirds would be back together before the weekend was out. He picked up the champagne bottle and refilled her glass. "When you just hear part of a conversation, it's easy to draw the wrong conclusion."

Josie shook her head. "This conversation left no other conclusion to be drawn. Robert gave a graphic account of his all-night exploits with the jump-out-of-the-cake girl from his bachelor party. When his friend said it was hard to believe he was finally going to settle down, Robert laughed and replied, 'Who said anything about settling down? As far as I'm concerned, getting married is nothing but a career move.'"

Josie placed her napkin on the table and pushed back her chair, shaking her head in disgust. "He only wanted to marry me so Dad would make him a partner. He didn't even try to deny it when I confronted him."

"You confronted him?"

Josie nodded. "I marched right into the room and told him I'd heard the whole conversation. He went white as a ghost. He begged for my forgiveness—and pleaded with me not to tell my father. Can you imagine the nerve?"

What was hard for Luke to imagine right now was any man preferring another woman over Josie. Her hair had dried into a mass of shiny, unruly curls that swayed when she moved her head, and her heart-shaped face was as sweet as a valentine, despite its indignant expression. Her eyes had the longest, silkiest lashes he'd ever seen on a human being, and they held him as enthralled as her story.

"What did you do?" he asked.

"Fortunately, my sister Sara had followed me into the hallway and heard the whole conversation—otherwise Robert probably would have tried to lie his way out of it. Sara helped explain things to my parents while I got the heck out of there. To avoid a scandal, it was agreed that the minister would announce that the wedding was postponed by mutual agreement."

Luke shook his head in amazement. "You've had quite a day."

Josie reached for her glass. "I'll drink to that."

For a person who'd been through such an ordeal, she sure seemed composed. But she'd left out a key element, Luke reflected: she hadn't said how she felt about the man. If she'd planned to marry him, she must have cared for him.

"What did you see in this guy in the first place?" Luke asked.

Josie had been asking herself the same question, and she didn't like the answers. They reflected too poorly on her decision-making abilities. They pointed out all too clearly how heavily she'd relied on the opinions of others, how little she'd trusted her own judgment.

She pushed out of her chair and crossed the room to the fireplace. Leaning against the mantel, she settled on a partial answer. "I honestly don't know."

Luke stood and joined her before the fire. His gaze was as warm on her face as the fire was on her back. "Was it just a physical thing?"

The question startled her so much she replied without thinking. "Oh, no. It wasn't physical at all."

"If you'd gone through with the ceremony, I imagine

things would be getting pretty physical right about now."
Luke's voice was tinged with sarcasm.

Josie gazed into the fire and swallowed hard. She hadn't
really allowed herself to think about *that* part of the marriage. Every time she'd started to wonder about it, her mind
had shut down, refusing to pursue the train of thought.
She'd told herself it would all work out when the time
arrived. Now she realized she'd avoided thinking about it
because the necessary feelings were missing.

"Surely you'd kissed him," Luke persisted.

"Well, yes, but there wasn't any—I mean—" Josie
swallowed once more. Her eyes locked on his lips as they
had in the barn, and again she felt that strong, magnetic
tug. "Nothing happened," she murmured in a voice at least
an octave lower than usual.

He stepped closer, his gaze trapping hers, "Nothing else
happened, or you felt nothing when you kissed him?"

"Yes. Both." Mercy, his eyes were sexy…so dark and
intense and probing. With a jolt she realized she was looking at a mirror image of the attraction unfurling in her belly.
She knew she should avert her gaze, but she couldn't pull
her eyes away.

Sparks flew between them, filling the air like the scent
of the cedar logs on the fire, raising the temperature of the
room. Her voice lowered to a husky whisper. "Nothing
ever happened."

But something was happening now.

Luke moved closer until he was standing directly in front
of her. The air all but disappeared from her lungs. A log
snapped on the fire, and heat blazed between them.

Attraction, hot and primitive and strong, curled between
them like smoke. A shiver snaked up Josie's arm and down
her spine. She knew she was staring, but she couldn't pull

her eyes away. If the building had caught fire, she doubted she could have moved to save her life.

The loud, impertinent ring of a telephone shattered the spell.

Luke strode across the room and jerked the phone off the table. "Hello?" he demanded.

Josie watched, dazed and jelly-kneed, her heart still racing like a runaway horse.

A scowl crossed his face. "One moment." He turned to Josie, his face stony, his eyes inscrutable, and thrust out the receiver. "It's for you. It's Robert."

Chapter Three

The next morning Josie pushed through the double oak doors from the lodge's dining room to the kitchen and found Consuela attacking a mound of dough with a rolling pin as she talked with a dark-haired man in rapid Spanish.

The housekeeper looked up, her smile as welcoming as the kitchen's warmth after the chilly predawn hike from the cabin. "Why, good morning, Miss Randall!"

Josie smiled back. "Good morning, Consuela. And please, call me Josie."

The housekeeper beamed and pointed the rolling pin at the middle-aged man behind her, who was as thin as Consuela was hefty. "Josie, I'd like you to meet my husband. Manuel helps Mr. Luke with the ranch."

"Nice to meet you."

"The pleasure's mine," he replied with a grin. "Hope you enjoy your stay." He gave Consuela a hearty kiss on the cheek. "Well, I'd better go see to the horses."

Consuela stopped rolling dough to kiss him back. Her

eyes were soft and affectionate as she watched him leave the room.

"Have you been married long?" Josie asked.

"Twenty-seven years."

"You still seem very much in love."

"*Si.* He's a wonderful man." She turned concerned eyes on Josie as she resumed her attack on the dough. "But how are you this morning? What are you doing up so early?"

Josie pulled her hands from the pockets of her plaid wool jacket and appreciatively inhaled the scent of baking bread and brewing coffee. "I'm fine. I'm an early riser, that's all. I saw a light on in here and came in search of coffee."

Consuela nodded amiably. "It's on the counter. Help yourself."

Josie selected an empty mug from a stack of cups near the pot and filled it with the fragrant, steaming brew. She looked around the kitchen, admiring the glazed brick floor, the cedar plank walls, the gleaming copper pots and pans. Despite its industrial-size appliances and sparkling stainless steel equipment, the kitchen had a homey, rustic charm.

Consuela's dark eyes were warm and intent as she regarded Josie. "Did you get any sleep?"

"I slept like a baby." Once she'd finished tossing and turning, Josie added silently.

"I was afraid you had too much on your mind to sleep well."

She'd had a lot on her mind, all right—but her thoughts had not been on the man Consuela supposed. Instead, she'd found herself strangely preoccupied with Luke. He'd marched out of the cabin after handing her the phone, leaving her alone to talk with Robert.

The conversation with her former fiancé had been brief. She'd had little to say, and when she'd hung up the phone, the only emotion she'd felt was relief.

Josie knew Consuela was waiting for an explanation. "I was exhausted. I'd lain awake most of the night before, wondering if I wasn't about to make a terrible mistake."

Surprise flickered across Consuela's broad face as she set down the rolling pin. "You didn't love this man you almost married."

Josie liked the matter-of-fact way she spoke the words, with no condemnation or judgment. "No."

The large woman cocked her head to the side, her brow furrowed. "So why were you going to marry him?"

Josie sighed and leaned against the kitchen counter, cradling the coffee cup in her palms, and gazed at Consuela. Her face was open and kind, and Josie decided to answer honestly. "Good question."

"Did you think you loved him?" the older woman asked gently.

"I wasn't sure." Josie curled her fingers around the warm mug and searched for the right words. "Robert works for my father, and he seemed to be everything a woman could want—smart, handsome, charming, on his way to becoming a big success. My three older sisters considered him a real prize, and my parents adored him. My family was so crazy about him that when I told them he'd proposed, they didn't even ask me what my answer was. They just immediately began making wedding plans. Everyone seemed so certain it was the right thing for me to do that I just went along with it."

"What were your feelings for him?"

Josie shrugged. "I liked him, I admired his intelligence, but beyond that... I didn't know. How are people supposed to feel if they're in love? Surely not everyone sees fireworks or rainbows." The memory of how she'd felt last night with Luke flashed through her mind, but she quickly shoved the thought aside. That had been nothing more than a reaction to the champagne and an emotionally charged state, she reasoned. "The bottom line is I didn't know if I loved Robert or not because I didn't know what love was supposed to feel like."

Consuela's eyes were sympathetic and knowing. "If you were really in love, you wouldn't have had any question. You would have just known."

Josie lifted her coffee cup and took a sip. "Well, there's one thing I know now—I'm awfully glad the wedding was called off. I feel like the weight of the world has been lifted from my shoulders."

"That's a sure sign you made the right decision." Consuela turned back to the biscuits. "You were fortunate. Luke wasn't so lucky."

"What do you mean?" Josie asked.

"He was engaged to the wrong person, too, but he went ahead and married her. He and Cheryl were married only two months before she left."

"How long ago was that?"

"Five years." Consuela arranged the biscuits on a baking sheet. "I keep telling that man he needs to get a wife."

For some reason the thought of Luke with another woman made Josie's stomach clench. "Does he have any prospects?"

Josie had tried to keep her voice casual, but Consuela's bright, dark eyes seemed to see right through her. The woman gave a small, Mona Lisa smile. "No. I think he's— what's the phrase? Goon-shy."

Josie smiled. "I think you mean gun-shy."

Consuela grinned back. "Maybe both, no?"

Josie laughed and nodded, all the while wondering why the information should make her stomach flutter. Uneasy at the way the housekeeper was scrutinizing her, she set down her coffee cup and pushed off the counter, anxious to change the topic.

"Do you do all the cooking here yourself? Don't you have any help?"

Consuela shook her head as she opened one of the double ovens and pulled out a tray of cinnamon rolls. She set them on a wire rack to cool, then slid the biscuits in to bake. "Ever since the last lodge manager left, we've had staffing trouble. Two girls are supposed to help in the kitchen in the mornings, but..." Consuela shrugged. "Sometimes they come late, sometimes they don't come at all. The evening shift is better, but not much. And the ladies who clean the guest rooms—" Consuela rolled her eyes "—it's a nightmare. Two quit last week. Mr. Luke has advertised for replacements, but for the time being, our hands are short."

Suppressing a smile, Josie took off her jacket, draped it over a chair and pushed up her sleeves. "I'd love to help. What can I do?"

Consuela shook her head. "Oh, no. You're a guest! You're here to relax, not to work."

"I'm not the type who enjoys sitting around and twiddling my thumbs," Josie insisted. She moved to the large, stainless steel sink and began washing her hands. "Besides, I worked as an assistant to the chef when I was taking a hotel training program and I'm pretty handy in a kitchen. I've missed it." Josie pointed to a bag of potatoes on the counter. "Let me guess. These need to be washed and peeled for hash browns."

"Yes, but..."

Josie pulled a potato scrubber out of a ceramic jar of implements, located a large empty bowl on the counter and dove into the task before Consuela could mount a protest. "I got the impression last night that Luke isn't too fond of the guest part of the guest ranch," Josie said as a diversion.

Consuela nodded and scooped some softened butter into a bowl. "He didn't want his father to build the lodge. They had a big argument, and Luke left the ranch. He only came back when his father was dying." Consuela's eyes grew sorrowful. "It was Mr. O'Dell's *corazon*—his heart, God rest his soul." She genuflected and gave a heavy sigh. "Now Luke has to run the lodge, and he hates it more than ever. He thinks his father worked himself to death over it. And it reminds him of the argument."

"Why does he keep it open?"

"He has to, for the ends to make the meat."

"I think you mean 'for ends to meet.'"

"*Si.*" Consuela nodded as she added powdered sugar and vanilla to the butter. "Mr. O'Dell mortgaged the ranch to build the lodge. Now Luke has to operate it to make the payments." She poured in heavy cream, then picked up a wooden spoon and stirred the ingredients together. "He's hired professional managers, but none of them have lasted more than a couple of months."

"Why not?"

"The first one was dishonest. The second one was—how do you say it?—incontinent."

Josie grinned. "Incompetent?"

"*Si.* The last one said there was no chance for advancement, and he took another job. That was over a month ago, and we're having a hard time finding a replacement." Consuela drizzled the freshly made icing over the cinnamon buns. "In the meantime, Luke's wearing both hats."

Josie was about to ask another question when the door pushed open and there Luke stood, his frame filling the doorway, holding one of those hats in his hand. It was a brown Stetson, and it looked as worn as his faded jeans and denim jacket. The sight of him made the butterflies she'd felt earlier metamorphose into bat wings.

Luke froze in the doorway as his eyes met hers. A nerve worked in his jaw. "I thought you'd be on your way back to Tulsa by now to kiss and make up."

Josie forced herself to continue calmly peeling the potato in her hand. "Why would you think a thing like that?"

"Because your fiancé called last night, and these little lovers' tiffs have a way of working themselves out."

"Wrong on three counts." Josie dropped the peeled potato into the bowl and picked up another spud, trying hard to hide the fact her pulse was unaccountably racing. "Robert is my *ex*-fiancé. And it wasn't a tiff."

"That's two. What's the third?"

Josie felt the color rise in her cheeks as she attacked the potato. For the life of her, she didn't want him to know how he rattled her. She tried to keep her voice cool, her tone offhanded. "We were never lovers, either."

Luke had surmised as much from their conversation last night, but he took an unexplained pleasure in hearing her say it. Not that it mattered to him, Luke thought. It made no difference to him either way.

It bothered him, though, to see her act as if the whole thing were over and done with—as if she had no feelings for the guy at all. He'd seen this behavior before. From his experience, the more a woman insisted she didn't care for a man, the more she actually did.

He tossed his hat on the seat of a ladder-back chair by the wall and shoved his hands in his pockets. "He must have meant something to you, if you were going to marry him."

"Her family pushed her into the engagement," Consuela chimed in. "She didn't really love him."

Startled, Luke jerked around to find Consuela on the opposite side of the kitchen, watching the exchange with undisguised interest. He'd been so focused on Josie he hadn't even registered the fact the housekeeper was in the room.

True to form, Consuela had wasted no time getting the inside scoop, Luke thought wryly. Hard to believe she'd fallen for Josie's I-never-loved-the-guy routine, though. She was usually so shrewd about these things.

How had Josie managed to snow her? Especially with such a phoney-baloney story. From what he'd seen of Josie, she wasn't the type who'd be easily coerced into anything.

Except maybe a kiss, Luke thought with a pang of guilt. It had sure been on his mind to try it last night. He ought to be ashamed of himself, entertaining thoughts like that about a woman in such a sad situation. It was a good thing the phone had rung when it did or he'd have had a hard time facing himself this morning.

His gaze darted back to Josie, and it suddenly registered that she was up to her elbows in potatoes. "What the heck are you doing?" he demanded.

"Peeling potatoes."

"I can see that. But why?"

"Because I wanted to make myself useful."

The most useful thing she could do was go back to Tulsa and leave him in peace, Luke thought grumpily. She'd stirred up thoughts and feelings he'd kept locked up for a good long while, and she'd all but ruined his night's sleep. "Thanks, but the kitchen is off-limits to guests. It's a lodge rule."

Josie dropped a peeled spud in the bowl and flashed that infuriating dimple, the one that had plagued his thoughts for half the night. "Everyone knows rules are made to be broken. Besides, I'm enjoying myself, and Consuela needs some help. This is too much work for one person."

"Well, then, I'll help her," Luke retorted.

Consuela rolled her eyes and threw up her hands. "Oh,

no! Last time you helped, it took me an extra hour to clean up the mess.'' She vigorously shook her head. ''Thanks, but no thanks.''

He rubbed the back of his neck, where a knot of tension was forming, and watched Josie calmly peel another potato. It was true Consuela needed assistance, and it was a proven fact he was all thumbs in a kitchen. There was no reason why Josie's helping out should bother him so.

Except that he wanted her to leave, and here she was, making herself at home, becoming thicker than thieves with Consuela.

Still, making a fuss did nothing but make him look as ill-tempered as a penned-up bull. ''Suit yourself,'' he muttered. Even to his own ears, it sounded like a particularly ingracious way to show appreciation for volunteer labor. ''Thanks for giving us a hand,'' he forced himself to add.

Consuela smiled warmly at Josie. ''Yes, thank you.'' She wiped her hands on her white apron. ''Now if you two will excuse me, I need to run to the cellar to get some onions for the hash browns.''

Luke plucked his hat from the chair as Consuela scurried from the room. After the way Josie had affected him last night, he had no intention of being alone with her again. ''I'll go see about pulling your car out of the mud,'' he said.

''There's no hurry,'' Josie replied, glancing up from the potatoes. ''I won't need it for a week.''

A weight sank and settled at the bottom of Luke's stomach like a thrown horseshoe. ''So you intend to stay.''

''I told you I wouldn't change my mind.''

Luke swallowed and forced his lips into a smile. ''Well, fine.'' Yeah, fine and dandy. He could look forward to a full week of raging testosterone. Even now, at five-thirty in the morning, he felt a pull of attraction to her.

He shifted his hat to his other hand and headed for the door. "Well, enjoy yourself. The activities schedule is posted in the dining room. The group trail ride leaves at ten."

Josie's eyebrows flew up. "Oh, I'm not going with the group. I'm supposed to have private trail rides as a part of my package."

Luke stopped in his tracks. She wasn't really going to insist on all that honeymoon stuff, was she? "That package is for *two* people."

"Why should that matter? I've paid for the whole thing."

"But...but it'll just be you and the trail guide." And the trail guide is Butch Avery, the most prolific womanizer in the county, he added silently. Butch considered anything in a skirt to be fair game—and the objective of his game was to see how many notches he could carve on his bedpost. Letting a vulnerable, heartbroken woman go off alone with Butch would be like letting a fox baby-sit a chicken.

Josie placed the bowl in the sink, flipped on the faucet and began rinsing the potatoes. "I've never been big on group activities. Besides, you told me yourself that all the guests this week are couples and I'd feel like a third wheel."

"But...but..."

Her spine visibly stiffened. "But what?"

Luke shifted his hat to the other hand. "Well, Josie, it's a little much to expect us to dedicate one of our staff members to just one guest."

"Is the whole ranch as understaffed as the lodge?"

"No..." Luke admitted.

She snapped off the faucet and whipped around. "So let me see if I've got this straight. If I had a man with me, it wouldn't be a problem. But since I'm by myself, you suddenly don't have the staff?''

Dadblast it! She'd twisted it all around. "Look, I'll be more than happy to refund the difference between our regular guest rates and the honeymoon package.''

"I don't want a refund. I want exactly the same experience I would have gotten if I'd come here with a husband. I refuse to have my life compromised because I'm not part of a couple." Josie fixed him with a heated glare. "You know, there's a term for what you're trying to do here. It's called *discrimination*.''

"Now, wait just a cotton pickin' moment!" Luke raked a hand through his hair and glared back.

She placed both hands on her hips, her eyes flashing. "Come to think of it, there's another term that applies, too. *Bait and switch*.''

The only thing he'd like to switch was her behind. Dammit, he was only trying to protect her, but he could just imagine her reaction if he attempted to explain it to her.

Well, if she was going to take this attitude, she deserved whatever she got. Luke clamped his hat on his head. "At the Lazy O, we aim to please," he said tersely. "I'll tell Butch to saddle up for a honeymoon ride.''

He only hoped Butch wouldn't take the instructions too much to heart.

The sun was high in the sky when Luke pulled up at the corral and switched off the engine of his pickup truck. Rolling down the window, he leaned out to watch Butch help Josie down from the roan mare named Petunia.

His mouth twisted in a scowl. Just as he'd predicted: Butch was all over her like a cow in clover. The cowboy's hands stayed on her waist far longer than necessary, and he stood so close to her he could probably smell her soft, flowery scent. The thought made Luke do a slow burn, which blazed into outright anger as he watched the cowboy run a hand down Josie's shapely backside just before he released her.

Luke slammed the door hard enough to rattle the truck windows and strode toward the corral, where Butch had begun unsaddling the mare.

"Enjoying yourselves?" Luke demanded.

Josie looked up, her blue eyes startled. "I loved the ride."

"Well, howdy there, boss," Butch drawled. "This little lady's real handy in the saddle."

And I bet you're just dying to find out how she is in the sack, Luke thought darkly. "Is that a fact," he replied curtly.

"Yes, sir. She's real taken with the ranch, too. I'm plannin' on takin' her on a tour of the place this afternoon. She wants to see the longhorn cattle you're breeding, and I thought I'd show her the canoe launch site, too." The gleam in Butch's eyes reminded Luke of a dog with a new bone.

"Sorry, Butch, but I've got an errand I need for you to run this afternoon."

"Can't you send someone else?"

"All the other hands are tied up today."

Butch ran his fingers through his wavy blond hair. "Well, maybe I can do it while Josie's at lunch."

Luke shook his head. "Afraid you'll have to go all the way to Tulsa to take care of this."

"What is it?"

Luke thought fast. "We're fencing off a portion of the back pasture, and I need some barbed wire."

Butch gave a relieved grin. "Oh, I can buy that in Tahlequah."

"Not this kind. Stop by the house in half an hour and I'll give you the specs." That should give him enough time to look up an obscure type of wire in one of his equipment catalogues, Luke thought.

Butch glanced at Josie. "I sure hate to let this little lady down."

"I don't mind exploring the ranch on my own," she said quickly.

Luke shook his head. "I can't let you do that. Our insurance prohibits unescorted guests from roaming the ranch."

"But the agenda for the first day of my package includes a tour," Josie protested.

Luke hesitated. He'd been so intent on getting her away from Butch's clutches that he hadn't thought that far ahead. He scuffed a cowboy boot in the dirt and hooked his thumb through a belt loop. "There's a group nature hike this afternoon," he ventured.

Josie's chin tilted upward. "You know how I feel about group activities."

Yeah, he did—and he secretly shared her sentiments. As much as it irritated him, he had to admit he admired the way she stood up for herself and insisted on getting what she wanted.

He met her gaze and was temporarily undone by the blue of her eyes. Those eyes made him want to find out what other things they might have in common, what else about her there was to admire. When she looked at him like that, it was hard to remember all the reasons he didn't want to get involved with her.

For starters, he reminded himself, this was supposed to be her honeymoon. She might not act like it, but he couldn't let himself forget for a moment that she had a freshly broken heart. She might have fooled Consuela with that cock-and-bull story about never having loved the guy, but he wasn't buying it. And if there was one thing he knew for sure, it was that he never wanted to be a stand-in for some other man again.

Besides, even if she weren't one of the walking wounded, she still lived in Tulsa. She was a city girl who thought a ranch was romantic, of all things. Not to mention the fact that she lived a two-hour drive away. He didn't have time for a long-distance romance, and there was no point in getting anything started that could only last a week. Unlike Butch, he wasn't the type for such a short-term fling. He was pretty sure she wasn't, either.

No, pursuing her was out of the question. If he had any sense at all, he'd avoid her like a pit of rattlesnakes.

"So who's going to take me on the tour?" she asked.

Dammit, he could just kick himself. He couldn't assign another ranch hand now because he'd just said everyone else was busy.

Instead of avoiding the pit, he'd jumped right in it. And those rattlers were closing in.

He tipped the brim of his hat and sighed. "I reckon that'll be me."

Chapter Four

Luke ground his pickup to a halt in front of the lodge shortly after the lunch hour and exhaled harshly, trying to tamp down his irritation. He had a dozen things he needed to do this afternoon, and playing tour guide to Little Miss Love-'Em-and-Leave-'Em-at-the-Altar wasn't one of them. How had he managed to get roped into this, anyway?

He drummed his fingers on the dashboard, shaking his head in disgust. He knew darn good and well how it had happened; he'd lassoed himself with his own damn lariat. He didn't know why the thought of Butch making time with Josie had made him see red, but it looked like he was going to spend the rest of the day paying for it. He'd already wasted the better part of an hour lining out the particulars of a fool's errand for the ranch hand to perform.

Might as well get on with it, he thought glumly, swinging his long legs out of the truck. The sooner he got this tour started, the sooner he could get it over with.

A heavy wool rug muffled the sound of his boots on the hardwood floor as he entered the main hall. It was a cavernous room with log walls, enormous paned windows and a high, beamed ceiling, a room where everything was larger than life and oversize. Its masculine dimensions and furnishings were in stark contrast to the lone, slender figure occupying it, spotlighted by a sunbeam in front of the gigantic stone fireplace.

He'd know that mop of dark, tousled curls anywhere. And if he'd failed to recognize her hair, there was no way he could have mistaken those jeans-clad curves—not after the way they'd teased his imagination all morning.

"Ready?" He practically barked the word, and it came out sounding more like an order than a question.

Josie whipped around, and the blue of her eyes hit him like a two-by-four, knocking the breath out of his lungs. The fact she had such a disconcerting effect on him irritated him all the more.

He jerked his head in the direction of the door. "My truck's parked outside. Thought we'd start the tour in the back pasture."

"If you don't mind, I'd like to start right here at the lodge."

Oh, for the love of horse feathers! The last thing he wanted to do was answer a bunch of questions about this blasted building. He opened his mouth to tell her as much, then abruptly shut it.

She's a paying customer, O'Dell, he reminded himself. And unless he wanted to hear more accusations about discrimination or false advertising, he'd better make sure she got her money's worth.

"All right." He reluctantly turned and swept his arm in a half circle. "This here's the main room. Down that hall is a game room, the lodge manager's office and two small meeting rooms that aren't used much. You know where the dining room and the kitchen are. The guest rooms are in the attached wing, and there's a heated pool on the terrace outside. There's a small apartment for the manager attached to the lodge on the other side. That's about it. Ready to move on?''

To his consternation, Josie burst out laughing. Luke knit his brow in a frown. "What's the matter?"

She shook her head. "You lift the phrase *whirlwind tour* to new heights."

"Well, you can look around the lodge anytime you want," Luke said defensively. "You don't need a guide for that."

"I wasn't asking about the floor plan."

"Then what the heck were you asking about?"

Josie's smile disarmed him. "For starters, I'm curious about the fireplace. Were the stones quarried locally?"

"I wasn't here when the place was built," he said curtly. "Can't help you there."

Consuela was right, Josie thought; Luke had no use at all for the lodge. He was positively chomping at the bit to get out of here as soon as possible.

For some perverse reason, she didn't want to let him. "What about the Indian rugs?" she asked, gesturing to the beautiful wool creations scattered over the polished wood floor. "Were they made by local tribes?"

Luke lifted a shoulder. "Don't know. Dad hired some high-falutin' interior designer to handle all the furnishings."

The answer disappointed her. She'd hoped to find some piece of Luke in the lodge, some clue to his personality, some glimpse of the man behind the scowl and Stetson.

She gestured to a large wall hanging above the fireplace. "Then I guess you know don't anything about this beautiful quilt, either."

Luke's gaze shifted to the faded quilt, and she was surprised to see the hard, guarded edge in his eyes soften. "Well, now, the quilt's a different story. My mother made that."

Both the answer and the change in his expression startled her. She gazed up at the worn quilt, taking in the intricate design of shooting stars combined with bows and arrows. It was a beautiful piece of work, a patchwork masterpiece in blue and burgundy and deep forest green, with touches of cream and gold. "She must have been a wonderful seamstress. I sew a little myself, but I've never had the nerve to tackle anything like this." Josie glanced at Luke. The light in his eyes as he gazed at the quilt transformed him, making him seem less intimidating, more approachable. And more appealing than ever.

Stop that, she warned herself. She turned her attention back to the quilt. "It's exquisite. I thought it was an antique."

Luke met her gaze and gave a crooked grin, and an unwanted ripple of attraction raced through her. "It just looks like one because I nearly wore it out. It pulled duty as a picnic blanket, a sleeping bag, a pup tent, a saddle blanket, a tepee—you name it."

"It was yours," Josie murmured, gazing back up at the beautiful handiwork. "Oh—I see your name stitched in the corner! And it looks like there's something else embroidered around the edge, but I can't read it from here. What does it say?"

"'Shoot for the stars.'"

"How wonderful!" Josie stared at it, her heart swelling with emotion. What a wonderful message for a mother to pass on to her child, she thought. How confidence building, how positive, how inspirational...

How different from the subliminal message of dependence her own parents had given her. She swallowed around a sudden thickness in her throat. "It must have been very special to you."

Luke gave a short nod. "I loved it to pieces—almost literally. It would be in shreds by now if Consuela hadn't confiscated it when I was sixteen. She said it was too beautiful to ruin and it wouldn't endure another round through the washer."

"A lot of work went into making it," Josie said, studying the unusual design. "A lot of love, too. I bet you could feel it when you wrapped it around you."

Luke briefly met her gaze, and the way the hard brown of his eyes melted to a soft chocolate did something funny to her stomach. "When Mom gave it to me, she told me that if I ever lost my way, to look up, and the stars would get me back on track."

Josie's chest constricted with emotion. "She wanted you to follow your dreams."

Luke gave a slight smile, making the fine lines at the corners of his eyes fan out like the tails of the shooting stars on the quilt. "You're a quicker study than I was. At the time, I thought she was talking about nighttime navigation." He glanced back up at the wall hanging. "After Mom died, I used to lie under that quilt at night and pretend she'd just tucked me in—that she wasn't really gone, that she was just across the hall, reading or sewing. It was the only way I could get to sleep for a couple of years."

Josie's eyes misted over, blurring her view of Luke's face. She started to reach out a hand to him, then pulled back, not knowing what to do or say, not knowing if she should offer comfort, not knowing how it would be received if she did. She thought about her own mother, and couldn't imagine what it would have been like to grow up without her. Her mother might drive her crazy with her hovering and overprotectiveness, but her love and care and nurture had been the core of her childhood.

The lump in her throat made it hard to speak. "Your father must have loved the quilt, too, to have made it the focal point of the lodge."

Luke's eyes grew shuttered and his lips tightened into a taut line. "My mother made other quilts, all of them beautiful. It surprised the heck out of me to find this one hanging here—especially since Dad knew how I felt about the lodge." He glanced at his watch and shifted his stance, suddenly uneasy. "It's getting late. Ready to move on?"

She nodded and followed him from the room, moved by the glimpse into Luke's painful childhood, touched by the fact that the hard-bitten cowboy had a secret, sentimental side.

Judging from the way he was charging toward his pickup now, he sure hadn't intended to reveal it. He probably regretted giving her any personal information about himself at all, she thought as she scurried after him.

She wondered why knowing that should make her all the more intrigued by him. She wondered why the mention of his father had made him lock up faster than a shopkeeper at quitting time, and why he resented the lodge so much.

She wondered how she could get him to tell her all about it.

As he stalked toward his truck, Luke was wondering a few things, too—mainly just what in tarnation had gotten into him. He yanked open the door for Josie, closed it the moment she'd settled on the seat, then strode around the truck, rubbing his jaw as he went. He wasn't the sort of man who went around spewing out personal information to every Tom, Dick and Harriet. Hell, he hardly ever talked about his mother, and he'd never told another living soul how he used to pretend she'd tucked him in. What the devil had possessed him to prattle on like that to Josie?

It was the woman's confounded eyes, he thought, withering his brow into a scowl as he hoisted himself into the driver's seat. Something about those big blue eyes made his lips flap like a shirt on a clothesline.

He risked a quick glance at her and found her eyes locked on him now, studying him quizzically. Luke's scowl darkened, a silent defense against the effect she was having on him. Unless he wanted to play a round of twenty questions, he'd better turn the conversational tables, and turn them fast.

He jammed the key into the ignition and started the engine. "Is Josie a nickname or your whole name?"

"It's short for Josephine," she said, pulling the seat belt over her shoulder and fastening it at her waist. Luke couldn't help but notice how the strap flattened her jacket between her breasts, accentuating her curves in a most distracting manner. "I'm named after my dad. I guess my parents gave up hope of having a boy when they had their fourth girl."

Josephine. The old-fashioned, feminine sounding name somehow fit her. "So you've got three sisters, huh? Do they all live in Tulsa?"

"Yes. Along with their husbands and children." She gazed at him curiously. "Are you an only child?"

"Yep. Always wished I had brothers or sisters." He'd volunteered the information without thinking, then immediately regretted it. The whole idea is to keep the conversation focused on her, he reminded himself sternly.

He jammed his foot on the accelerator, and the truck jerked forward. "So you were the baby."

"And always will be, as far as my family's concerned."

A note of resignation in her voice made Luke cast her a curious glance. "You make that sound like a problem."

"Being the youngest has a downside," she said ruefully.

"Really? What's that?"

Josie brushed a strand of hair away from her face and sighed. "Well, with three bossy older sisters and a pair of overprotective parents, I've always had someone telling me what to do and what not to do. I never got much of a chance to make many of my own decisions when I was growing up." Her voice trailed off as she stared out the window. "So I guess it's no wonder I'm not too great at it now."

"What do you mean?"

"According to my family, all the major decisions I've ever made have turned out to be mistakes."

The conversation was probably getting too personal, but Luke couldn't resist delving just a little further. "Like what?"

"Well, my family has a tradition of practicing law. Seems like all the Randalls from the beginning of time were attorneys. My father worked in his grandfather's law firm, and Granddad worked in his father's firm—you get the picture. It was expected that I'd join the family firm or at least marry someone who had. So when I decided to major in hotel and restaurant management in college instead of pursuing a law degree, everyone was convinced I was making a terrible mistake. Moving to Chicago instead of staying in Tulsa was viewed as even worse."

Luke guided the truck through a thick stand of autumn-tinged woods and glanced at Josie in the dappled light of the overhead branches. "Those sound like personal choices, not mistakes."

"I thought so, too, at the time. But when I was out of a job in Chicago and couldn't land another one to save my life, it began to look like I should have followed my family's advice. I came back to Tulsa with my tail between my legs like a whipped puppy, with zero confidence in my own judgment. I figured my family must have been right—the logical thing for me to do was to work in the family firm, marry someone from a similar background, have a life like my sisters. After all, I was the only one in my family who was different, and I was the only one who seemed to be making a mess of things.'' Josie exhaled a heavy sigh. ''Unfortunately, feeling that way made me especially vulnerable to their next piece of advice.''

Consuela's earlier remark about Josie's family pressuring her into marriage suddenly fell into place. ''Let me guess. Marrying Robert?''

Josie nodded grimly, gazing out the window at the open pasture. ''They were all so sure he was Mr. Right, so excited when he proposed to me, so full of congratulations and plans that I—well, I guess I just let myself get swept along with the tide.'' She heaved a dejected sigh. ''Pretty wimpy, huh?''

Luke's mind flashed back to his own wedding five years ago, and a wave of empathy surged through him. He, too, had had second thoughts after he'd popped the question, but instead of addressing his concerns, he'd tried to tell himself his feelings were nothing more than typical prewedding jitters. He realized now that he should have paid a lot more attention to his cold feet, but at the time he'd been too caught up in shuffling them toward the altar.

''Actually, it's pretty understandable,'' he found himself responding. ''Wedding plans have a way of making you feel like you're racing downhill on a runaway locomotive, with no way of stopping the train or jumping off.''

''They sure do,'' she agreed emphatically.

He glanced over at her, and she gave a soft smile. It seemed to Luke that the truck cab had suddenly shrunk, that they were somehow closer than they'd been a moment ago. He turned his eyes back to the road, but not before he'd caught the glimmer of curiosity in her gaze.

"Sounds like you've had some experience along these lines yourself," she remarked.

"Afraid I have."

"What happened?"

Luke shrugged. "Cheryl was more interested in getting married than in being married."

"Why?"

"She was on the rebound. She'd had her heart broken, and she wanted to retaliate. I don't think she even knew what she was up to herself, but her whole motivation was to make her old flame jealous."

"Oh, Luke! That must have been awful for you."

Luke rubbed his jaw. "Hurt my pride something awful, I'll say that. Made me feel like the dumbest country bumpkin that ever fell off the turnip truck. But in retrospect, she did me a huge favor by leaving. She wasn't the type of woman I would have wanted to be saddled with for the long haul."

"Had you known her long?"

"Yes…and no. I went to high school with her. She moved here from Dallas my junior year. She was the town beauty, the girl all the guys fantasized about. Probably because she seemed so unattainable."

"Why was that?"

He was talking too much. The wise course of action would be to just shut up, but Josie's gaze was riveted on his face, and something about her enthralled expression made him ramble on like a tape recorder with a jammed Play button.

"Cheryl was a real ice queen. She wouldn't have anything to do with any of the local boys—said she liked the sophisticated, big-city type. She wouldn't give me the time of day in high school, and afterward she moved back to Dallas. I hadn't seen her in seven years. Then out of the blue, she called me up and said she'd been thinking about me, that we should get together. One thing led to another, and—Bam!—two months later we were married." Luke gave a wry grin. "Of course, two months after that, we were divorced."

"What a terrible experience," Josie murmured.

"After I got a little distance from the situation, I realized my ego was bruised a whole lot more than my heart. All the same, it's not an experience I care to repeat." Luke shook his head. "I served my time as a married man, and I don't intend to ever wear that ball and chain again."

How the heck had the conversation gotten off on this topic, anyway? Luke raked a hand through his hair and frowned in consternation. There he'd gone again, shooting off his big mouth, volunteering information about himself he'd had no intention of sharing with her.

It was more than her eyes that made him blather like a jaybird, he decided; it was that intent expression on her face. He didn't know when anyone had seemed so interested in something he'd had to say. She made him feel downright fascinating, and the attention went right to his head.

The thought made his scowl deepen, and he yanked the steering wheel harder than he needed to in order to miss a rut in the road. Josie bounced against him, her arm brushing his chest, and the contact sent a disturbing rush of warmth shooting through him.

He spotted a herd of cows as he topped the hill ahead and exhaled in relief, glad for an excuse to extricate himself from the conversation and the suddenly too-intimate confines of the truck.

"I need to check a calf with a cut leg in that herd." He pulled the pickup to a halt, killed the engine and thrust open his door. "I'll toss out a few bales of hay, take a look at her leg and be right back."

"I'll come with you." Josie clambered out before Luke could voice an objection. A dozen brown-and-white cows ambled toward them, mooing plaintively. "Looks like they're glad to see you," Josie said.

"It's not me they're glad to see. It's their lunch." Luke opened the tailgate, climbed in the truck bed and tossed out a bale of hay. The cows clustered around, scooped up huge, messy mouthfuls and chewed, eyeing them dispassionately.

"Is that all you're going to give them to eat?"

He glanced at the cows. As far as he could tell, they were the very picture of bovine bliss. His eyebrows quirked upward. "What else do you think they want?"

"I thought you fed them cow chips."

"Cow chips?" Luke stared at her. "What the dickens are you talking about?"

"Well, Butch told me he'd once won the cow chip throwing contest at a heritage festival, and I was hoping to see some. I wondered what they looked like."

Luke's jaw fell slack with disbelief. "You're wondering what a cow chip looks like?"

Josie nodded.

A smile twitched at the corner of his mouth. He rubbed his jaw to try to hide it. "What do you *think* they look like?"

She shrugged. "I don't know. Potato chips or corn chips or—"

Luke couldn't keep the laughter from erupting from his throat. "I don't quite know how to tell you this, Josie, but a cow chip deals with the other end of the cow than you're imagining." He glanced down at the ground and widened his grin. "And if you don't watch out, you're about to step on one."

Josie's gaze flashed to her feet. She stared for a moment, then looked up at Luke, her eyes were wide and horrified. "*That's* a cow chip?"

Luke nodded, his face creased in an ear-splitting grin.

"People throw *that?*"

Luke let out a chortle. "When they get old and dry, they're as hard as a piece of wood. In fact, in the western part of the state where trees are scarce, the early settlers used them as firewood."

Josie's face crinkled in distaste. "I wouldn't want to toast my marshmallows over *that.*"

Luke threw back his head and roared. To his surprise Josie joined him, laughing until tears pooled at the corners of her eyes.

Good gravy, she was lovely, Luke thought, watching her. And her laughter was one of the nicest sounds he'd ever heard—rich, real, earthy, contagious. He laughed with her until long moments later, when she drew a ragged breath, wiped her eyes and grinned up at him.

"You must think I'm the greenest greenhorn you've ever seen, huh?"

But that was not what Luke was thinking at all. He was far too busy drinking in the sight and sound and smell of her, far too preoccupied fighting the urge to pull her in his arms and kiss her silly.

He gave himself a mental shake, but he couldn't wipe the smile off his face. And he couldn't resist teasing her further. He jammed a thumb in the pocket of his jeans and grinned. "Well, that depends."

"Depends on what?"

"On whether or not you thought I was going to serve those cow chips with sheep dip."

She leaned against him and laughed until her knees buckled. His arm somehow made its way around her shoulders, and when they stopped laughing and looked at each other, they were standing close enough that he could smell her perfume, feel the heat of her body, see the dark blue facets radiating out from the pupils of her eyes.

Attraction crackled between them, electrifying the air. Luke gazed at her, dazzled by a riot of optic impressions. The sunshine streamed through her hair, streaking it with red and gold highlights, reflecting the blazing color of the autumn leaves behind her. A faint dusting of freckles danced across her nose. Her cheeks were pink and wind kissed, her lips soft and upturned and tempting.

The combined effect made Luke feel like his senses were on overload, about to short-circuit. When her eyes met his, a jolt of emotional energy surged between them, and it seemed like the most natural thing in the world for his head to lower toward her waiting lips.

The moment he did, he felt like he'd stepped on a downed power line, like the world had exploded under his feet. Nothing mattered, nothing existed except the sweet, urgent heat of her mouth on his. Her lips yielded and parted, and he pulled her against him, winding an arm around her back, tangling a hand in her hair, losing himself in the exquisite sensation of her mouth moving with his.

Desire, hot and intense, pulsed through him. Her arms clutched his back as if she were holding on to him for dear life, and then—

Something wet nudged his backside. Jumping as if he'd been gigged by a cattle prod, he jerked around to find the half-grown heifer he'd come to check out nosing the back pocket of his jeans.

The interruption struck him like a pitcher of cold water. He pulled away from Josie, jammed his hand in the pocket the calf was nuzzling and extracted a peppermint. The calf's velvety muzzle claimed it from the flat of his hand.

Luke reached back in the pocket, pulled out a handful of peppermints and thrust them at Josie. "Here. In lieu of cow chips, why don't you give her some of these while I check that cut on her leg."

Luke crouched beside the calf, glad for a duty to perform, aroused and upset and thoroughly disgusted with himself.

Dammit, he didn't need this kind of distraction. He had a ranch to run and a lodge to manage. He didn't have time to be conducting tours or drumming up wild-goose chases or getting as steamed up as a shaving mirror in the middle of the day. Especially over a woman who'd just confirmed all his suspicions that she was the rankest rank amateur who'd ever set foot on the Lazy O.

Cow chips, indeed! He looked up from the calf's leg to find Josie watching him, her blue eyes wearing a slightly dazed expression, her lips pink and kiss swollen, her cheeks brighter than the weather alone explained.

He swallowed hard, fighting back the urge to pick up right where they'd just left off. He needed to explain his actions, but he'd be damned if he knew what the explanation was.

He slowly straightened, taking care to keep the calf between them, then stared down at his boots and cleared his throat. "Look, I didn't mean to get out of line just now," he mumbled. "I don't exactly know what happened. I guess I was laughing too hard and just got overly ex...ex—" Oh, criminy, O'Dell—say anything except *excited!* "Exuberant."

Overly exuberant. Oh, that was a good one. Flyin' catfish—where the heck had he come up with that?

Josie's cheeks flamed. Luke swallowed painfully and

averted his eyes. "Anyway, I'm sorry. It won't happen again." He motioned brusquely toward the truck. "We'd better get going. We've got a lot of ground to cover."

He stalked toward the pickup, wishing some of that ground would just open up and swallow him now.

Chapter Five

Josie braced her hand on the dashboard as the pickup bumped its way back toward the lodge late in the afternoon. The setting sun lit the clouds like a brushfire, blazing the sky with color brilliant enough to rival the surrounding autumn foliage, but Josie was too focused on the man beside her to pay much attention to the passing scenery.

Luke was staring straight ahead, his face such a study of concentration that he might have been navigating a course of land mines.

Ever since they'd left the cow pasture, he'd been rigid and stiff and withdrawn. Not that he'd been rude; on the contrary, Josie reflected, he'd been the epitome of politeness. He'd courteously answered all her questions about the ranch. He'd dutifully shown her the crop of winter wheat, the herd of longhorn cattle, the quarter horse breeding stables. In response to her questions, he'd perfunctorily explained that he held an animal husbandry degree from Oklahoma State University, that ranching was a business

as well as a way of life, that technology played a key role
in his operation.

Under any other circumstances, she would have been impressed with the size of the Lazy O, with the scope of the
operation, with Luke's scientific approach to managing it.

But she'd been far too impressed by the heart-stopping
way he'd kissed her in that cow pasture to register much
of an impression about anything else.

Eyeing his rigid profile now, it was hard to believe he'd
behaved with such spontaneity and passion. She might even
be inclined to think she'd imagined the whole thing, except
for the fact that nothing in her experience equipped her to
imagine anything like that toe-curling kiss. She'd never felt
anything like it, never knew such sensations actually existed. The memory made her mouth dry, and her pulse fluttered in her throat.

For the life of her, she didn't know how it had started.
One minute they'd been boisterously laughing, and the next
his gaze had fastened on hers. Then his eyes had gone all
smoky and dark, and his face had tilted and lowered, and
his mouth had gotten that intent, hungry set as it moved
closer and closer to hers, almost in slow motion, until their
lips had finally met.

Josie swallowed hard and gazed out the window, getting
that funny, melting sensation in her stomach all over again
at just the thought of it.

There was no denying that kiss had happened. Even more
shocking, there was no denying how much she'd enjoyed
it—or how thoroughly she'd kissed him back.

Shaken, she turned her head and stared out the passenger
window. She'd only responded that way because her emotions were in a state of upheaval, she told herself fiercely.
It must have been some kind of warped reaction to the fact
that she was on a honeymoon alone.

It couldn't have been anything else. She wasn't in the market for a romance right now; that would be like jumping out of the frying pan into the fire. No, she was just in an emotionally heightened state and she'd overreacted, that was all.

Not that Luke didn't have several attributes that might make any woman overreact, a traitorous little voice in her head piped up. The way he looked, for example. She sneaked a glance at his profile, taking in the squareness of his beard-shadowed jaw, the deep cleft in his chin, the fine lines etched at the edges of his eyes. She had to admit that there was a rugged, basic maleness about him that was undeniably sexy.

And the way he'd handled that hurt calf, his big hands running down its injured leg as gently as a dewdrop on a blade of grass—that was sexy, too. So was the sentimental side he'd inadvertently let her see when he'd talked about that quilt.

But sexiest of all was the way he'd responded when she'd explained how her family had nearly railroaded her into marriage. He'd not only been understanding and sympathetic, but he'd opened up and let her see that he, too, had been foolish in matters of the heart. His willingness to tell her how he'd made a similar mistake had touched her. Behind his rough, tough exterior, Luke was kind and decent and compassionate. And in her opinion, nothing made a man sexier than that.

He glanced over and caught her staring at him. Their eyes locked and held, and an unwelcome jolt of electricity again raced through her. He jerked his eyes back to the windshield. Her face on fire, she simultaneously did the same.

There it was again—that jarring, kinetic connection. Josie drew a deep breath and tried to reason her galloping pulse rate back down to a trot.

Okay, so there was some kind of attraction between them. It didn't change the fact that the timing was all wrong. She had other priorities to address. And judging from Luke's stilted behavior, he didn't want a romantic involvement right now any more than she did.

But all of her cool, logical thinking did nothing to ease the unbearable tension sizzling between them. She searched her mind for something, anything, to say to break the silence. "Are we getting close to the lodge?"

"Just over this hill."

They both exhaled huge sighs of relief when the rustic wood and stone building finally loomed into view. The moment the truck rolled to a stop, Luke leapt out, rounded the vehicle and opened her door.

Josie climbed down, careful to avoid touching him. She didn't want to aggravate the hot, heady sensation that was already muddling her thinking. "Thanks for showing me around."

"Don't mention it." He touched the brim of his Stetson and gave a curt, polite nod. "If you'll excuse me, I need to go check a few things at the barn."

Josie watched the truck rattle off down the road, wondering why the sight of its retreating tailgate should leave her feeling lost and a little forlorn.

She turned toward the lodge, where the other guests were milling around. Sure enough, just as Luke had warned her when she'd first arrived, all of the other guests were couples. Not just ordinary couples, either—affectionate, cozy couples. Heck, Josie thought dourly, they all looked like honeymooners, as paired off as turtle doves. An older couple was seated on a bench under the fiery red leaves of a maple tree, deep in conversation, holding hands. A younger man and woman meandered through the trees in the distance. Two couples were laughing and playing horseshoes in a clearing across the road, and yet another pair leaned against each other on the porch, reading a book together.

A stab of loneliness shot through Josie. She felt as out of place as a mouse at a cat convention. Maybe Luke and her parents were right. Maybe coming here alone was a lousy idea.

No, she told herself firmly. She'd made a decision to come here, and she was going to stick to it. If she was ever going to learn to trust her own judgment, she had to stop second guessing herself and start sticking by her decisions.

She'd begun to climb the wooden porch steps when the lodge door opened. "Well, hello, there," a familiar voice called.

Josie glanced up to find Butch swaggering toward her, his hand looped on his wide-buckled belt.

"Hello," she responded, suppressing a grimace. She had no use for men with smooth lines or smooth moves, and both of Butch's were slick as an oil spill. His practiced compliments, sly innuendoes and lingering touches had nearly ruined her trail ride this morning. She'd been glad Luke had sent him to Tulsa for the afternoon and spared her from having to endure any more of his company.

Butch gave a slow, practiced grin, showing a row of gleaming white teeth. Josie was sure he considered his smile irresistible. Maybe other women did, too, but she found it as pompous and calculating as the man himself.

"Mighty fine evenin'," he drawled. "Care to take a stroll?"

"No, thanks. I'm on my way in to help Consuela."

Judging from the way Butch's eyebrows rose in surprise, he was unaccustomed to being turned down. She scooted into the lodge before he could press her further, taking secret satisfaction in his displeased expression.

"Maybe I'll see you after dinner," he called after her.

Not if I see you first, she thought, firmly closing the door behind her.

She found Consuela in the dining room, arranging silverware on the gingham-checked tablecloths. Out the wide picture window, Butch sulkily strode to a dusty Chevy.

Consuela tilted her head in the direction of the retreating cowboy. "He's been lying in wait for you."

"Butch?"

Consuela nodded. "He thinks he's quite the ladies' man."

"Well, this is one lady who has no use for him. Or any other man, for that matter."

Consuela inclined her head. "They're not all like that one. You need a good man like my Manuel."

Josie gave a wan smile. "Maybe someday I'll be as lucky as you. But right now I need a good, long, cooling-off period before I even think about getting involved again."

Consuela gave a wry smile. "From what you told me about your relationship with your fiancé, there was nothing to cool off from."

Josie couldn't keep from laughing. "That's true. Things weren't so hot between us."

"I saw Luke drive off just now," Consuela remarked, her tone a little too offhanded. "And he didn't look very cool."

Mercy, the woman was perceptive! Josie felt her face color. Hoping to hide it, she snatched up a handful of silverware from the sideboard, ducked her head and began setting a table.

"The two of you seemed to strike sparks off each other

this morning." Consuela stopped and looked at her pointedly. "He's the kind of man you need to look for, Josie."

Josie fumbled the silverware, and a spoon noisily clanged to the hardwood floor. She bent to retrieve it, trying to retrieve her composure, as well. When she straightened, she decided to reply just as directly as Consuela had spoken. "Romance isn't on my priority list right now. I want to make sure I can trust my own judgment before I get involved with a man again." She placed a fork beside a folded gingham napkin. "Besides, from what I've seen of Luke, he's not in the market for a relationship, either."

"Love isn't something you plan," the older woman said, shaking her head sagely. "It happens in its own time, in its own way. Usually when you least expect it, when you're focused on something else."

Josie's thoughts inadvertently flew to the sparks she'd felt with Luke that afternoon. She deliberately thrust the disturbing memory aside. "Well, the thing I need to focus on right now is getting my life in order, and the first step is getting my career on track. Helping you here at the lodge is good practice. How can I help with dinner?"

Later that evening, after most of the guests had retired to their rooms and Consuela had headed home, Josie started down the trail to her cabin, carrying a plate of food. Against the housekeeper's objections, she'd spent the entire evening in the kitchen. She'd had no desire to dine alone in a roomful of couples, and she hadn't much wanted to mingle with them afterward, either. Besides, staying busy kept her from thinking about Luke and that disturbing, mind-bending kiss.

She gazed up at the nearly full moon as her footsteps crunched on the leaf-strewn pathway, and deliberately steered her thoughts away from him. She'd come here to

think about her future, and that was what she intended to
do.

What she'd told Consuela earlier was true, Josie reflected
as she walked through the crisp night air. The key to rebuilding her life was rebuilding her career. Her temporary
job at her father's firm was at an end, and she wanted to
stand on her own two feet now, independent of her family.

Reference or no reference, she needed to figure out a
way to land another job in her chosen field. Working with
Consuela had reinforced how much she enjoyed the hospitality industry and how much she'd missed it. Her career
choice was the biggest decision she'd ever made entirely
on her own, and if she were ever to develop confidence in
her own judgment, she needed to prove to herself that it
wasn't the mistake her family seemed to think it was.

A twig cracked sharply on the path ahead of her. Someone was approaching. Peering through the darkened trees,
Josie made out the silhouette of a cowboy hat perched atop
a tall, masculine form.

Oh, great—Butch. Josie stifled a moan. The last thing
she wanted to deal with tonight was another round of his
unwelcome attention. She wanted to spend the evening
sorting out her thoughts in peace and quiet, not fending off
the advances of an overly amorous cowpoke.

If he didn't see her, she wouldn't have to deal with him.
The thought was enough to make her rapidly scramble off
the path and duck behind a boulder.

She felt more than a little ridiculous as she crouched
behind the rock, balancing the warm plate of barbecued ribs
and beans against her chest. Her legs began to cramp as
long minutes passed. Crickets chirped, a bullfrog croaked,
and the wind rustled in the leaves, but no other sounds
broke the stillness of the night.

He must have turned around and gone the other way, she

finally decided. With a sigh of relief, she stood and straightened.

"Hold it right there, buster," ordered a deep, terse voice from the woods behind her.

Her heart in her throat, Josie screamed and threw up her hands. Her plate went flying.

"What the hell—"

She knew that voice. It had greeted her in the very same way when she'd first arrived at the ranch.

"Luke!" Josie gasped. She whipped around to find him standing behind her. By the dim light of the moon, she could see baked beans dripping from the brim of his hat. Her hand flew to her mouth. "What…what are you doing?"

"I was about to ask you the same question." The scowl on his face could have boiled a vat of tar. "What the devil are you doing, lurking behind a rock in the middle of the night?" He yanked the hat off his head and stared at it. "And what the heck did you just throw on me?"

"M-my dinner."

Luke gazed from his hat to her, his face a study of disbelief. "Why in blazes did you do that? Just what the hell is going on?"

Josie stared back, searching wildly for a response. She couldn't bring herself to tell him she was avoiding Butch. After all, the man was a flirt, not a threat, and mentioning it to Luke would make it seem like a bigger deal than it was. Besides, she didn't want Luke to think she couldn't handle herself with a flirtatious ranch hand.

She could. Why, she could even handle herself with him.

She lifted her chin, fighting off the old sense of inadequacy that always overtook her whenever she'd made a mistake. If she wanted to spend the whole night behind that rock, it was her own business, she thought stubbornly. She was a grown woman, and she didn't have to explain her every move. Not to him, anyway.

At least, not accurately. "I was going to my cabin, and I heard a...a—" she thought fast "—an owl. I was hoping to see it."

"You were out here *bird-watching?*" Luke's voice was incredulous.

Josie was glad of the dark, because it made it easier to avoid meeting his eyes. She'd always been a lousy liar. "Y-yes."

"At *night?*"

"Well, when else would you expect to see an owl?"

Luke looked far from satisfied with the explanation. He stared at her suspiciously, then glanced down at his hat. A rib was sticking up near the crown like a feather. He plucked it off and tossed it on the ground, shaking his head and muttering under his breath. Josie caught the phrase *city slickers* and was glad she couldn't hear the rest of his mumbled remark.

"Whatever you were up to, hiding in the woods at night was a damn fool stunt," he growled. "All I saw was someone ducking behind a rock, and I thought I'd stumbled onto some kind of crook. I had no idea it was you. Lots of folks around here would shoot first and ask questions later. Why, I nearly coldcocked you myself."

Josie straightened her back. Everyone made occasional errors, she told herself fiercely. It didn't mean she was fundamentally flawed, and it didn't mean Luke had the right to intimidate her. She pulled herself to her full stature and regarded him with as much dignity as she could muster. "I'm sorry I alarmed you, and I'm sorry about your hat, but there's no need to act so surly about it." Her gaze slid down, and her frosty demeanor melted as she realized beans were dripping off his denim jacket. "Oh, dear—I've gotten food all over your jacket, too!'' She reached out and tried to brush it off. His chest was rock hard under her hand, and the feel of it sent a shiver up her arm that had nothing to do with the chill night air.

Luke pulled away from her touch as if he'd been burned. The last thing he needed right now was more physical stimulation. He'd been miserably overstimulated ever since this confounded woman had hit the ranch.

Something about her touch made him soften his tone, however. "My clothes will be all right. Believe me, they've seen worse."

He gazed down at her and was struck by how pale her small, heart-shaped face looked in the moonlight. She certainly didn't look like the evil-minded, spell-casting, she-devil he'd built her up to be in his mind. She looked delicate and feminine and worried, and looking at her made something inside him melt like a candy bar in the summer sun.

A pang of guilt shot through him. Hell, it wasn't her fault he'd lost control of himself this afternoon. He was the one who'd instigated that kiss, and it wasn't fair of him to try to shift the blame to her.

He needed to lighten up and start treating her like the paying guest she was. He jammed his hands in his pockets and shifted his stance. "If I'm wearing your dinner, you must still be hungry. Might as well come on back to the lodge and fix another plate. I was heading there to get something to eat myself."

Her smile made him give one back, loosening a tightness he hadn't even known he had in his chest.

"Okay. Thanks."

He glanced down at her as they started back toward the lodge. "Why didn't you eat earlier with the other guests?"

"I was helping Consuela in the kitchen."

Luke frowned. The idea of her getting too tight with the housekeeper disturbed him almost as much as the thought of her getting too deeply involved in the workings of the lodge. "I appreciate your help, Josie, but you really don't need to pull KP duty. We have a part-time cook who fills in on Consuela's days off, and we have two girls who assist her in the evenings."

"I know. But one of them didn't show up tonight."

Luke stifled an oath. "Again?"

"Consuela said you'd been having staffing problems ever since the last lodge manager left."

"That's true, but it's nothing for you to worry about. You're a guest here, and you shouldn't be spending all your time in the kitchen."

Josie waved a hand. "I'm enjoying it. Besides, I won't be in the kitchen tomorrow night. I'm scheduled for the evening trail ride and cookout."

Luke winced. He'd forgotten all about that. Damn, damn and double damn! He couldn't let her go off alone on a romantic nighttime outing with the likes of Butch. He made a mental note to line up Manuel or one of the other hands to escort her.

The kitchen door creaked as Luke opened it and followed Josie inside. He tossed his hat on a chair and watched her take off her windbreaker. There ought to be a law against the things her body did to a loose-fitting pink sweater and a pair of jeans, he thought. His mouth went dry as he took in the gentle curves of her breasts, the taper of her waist and the soft swell of her hips.

She looked up, and he jerked his eyes away, not wanting to be caught staring.

"If you take off your jacket, I'll see if I can undo some of the damage I caused," she said.

He'd have to take off more than his jacket in order for

her to do that, he thought ruefully. Aggravated at himself and the direction of his thoughts, he shrugged out of the bean-soaked denim and handed it to her, then strode across the room and yanked open the refrigerator. He pulled out a plate of ribs and three large, covered bowls and put them on the counter, then turned and watched her dab at his jacket with a damp cloth.

"That refund offer still stands, you know," he blurted out.

She looked up, her eyes wary. "What do you mean?"

"Well, now that you've seen the place, you can see there's not really that much to do. Not nearly enough to occupy you for a full week."

Josie's expression turned as ominous as a thundercloud. "You might as well give up trying to get rid of me. That discrimination routine didn't work before, and it won't work now."

"I'm not trying to discriminate against you!"

"Is there some other reason you want me to leave?"

"No. Of course not." *Unless you count the effect you're having on my temperature, my pulse rate and a few other bodily functions.* Luke reached into the cabinet and jerked a couple of plates off the shelf. They rattled against each other noisily and clanged when he set them down too hard on the countertop. "It's just that, well, you seem to be hiding out here in the kitchen, and you don't want to mingle with the other guests, and I thought..." He ran a hand through his hair and tried to think of a diplomatic way to put it. "I just thought you might be more comfortable back in Tulsa, that's all, and I wanted to let you know I'd be more than happy to give you your money back."

Josie's gaze was warmer, but still held an edge of suspicion. "Thanks, but I intend to stay through the rest of the week."

Luke tried to keep the frustration out of his voice. "Would you mind telling me why?"

"You mean aside from the fact the ranch is beautiful and the facilities are lovely and the food is great?"

"Yeah, aside from all that."

"Because I made up my mind to come here, and I'm going to stick by my decision."

Luke struggled to tamp down his frustration. "That's no kind of reason."

Josie's chin took on a stubborn tilt. "It is to me."

"And why on earth is that?"

She planted her feet apart and placed her hands on her hips. "Because all my life I've doubted my own decisions, and it's high time I started believing in myself. I nearly married the wrong man because I relied too heavily on my family's advice, and I'm not going to ever be that easily manipulated again. From here on out, I'm going to trust my own judgment. When I make up my mind about something, no one's going to talk me out of it."

Luke studied the stubborn set of her jaw and rubbed his own. Under the circumstances, he guessed her reaction was understandable. In a grudging way he even respected her for it. Heck, he thought, he was pretty much that way himself. If a person tried to make him budge on an issue, he'd usually dig in like a burr on a dog.

But understanding her reasons for staying didn't make the situation any better. If anything, it made it worse. Because now it looked like nothing short of a natural disaster was going to make her leave.

Josie picked up the damp cloth and resumed working on his jacket. "Besides, I've been living with my parents ever since I moved back to Tulsa, and I'd just as soon let things settle down before I have to deal with them. They're going to want to smother me with TLC and advice, and the last thing I want right now is smothering.'' Josie gave the jacket a final wipe, then shook it out and draped it over the back of a chair. ''So I plan to stay here and let my family calm down while I sort things out and try to figure a way to land another job at a hotel or a resort. In fact, I was wondering if you'd mind letting me use the computer in the lodge office tomorrow. I'd like to update my résumé.''

The request startled him. He'd never figured out how to use his father's equipment, but that didn't mean no one else should. It was just sitting there collecting dust. ''Well, sure.''

Her smile seemed connected to the electrical wiring, because when she flashed that dimple at him, Luke could swear the room became brighter and warmer. He deliberately turned away and began rummaging in a drawer for silverware in an effort to dim the reaction he was having to her. He might as well face it, he thought grimly. It looked like she was here for the duration.

But heck, it was just six more days. Surely he could handle that. Especially if he took precautions to make sure he didn't find himself alone with her again. A man could only take so much, and he couldn't stand too many more episodes like the one this afternoon.

He would just have to be careful to avoid potentially volatile situations. That cookout tomorrow night, for example. No way in Sam Hill was he going to escort her on that. He'd get Manuel or Jack or even old Ben, who was blind as a bat in the dark.

But there was no way in tarnation he was going to find himself alone with her on a moonlight trail ride.

Chapter Six

"Ready?" Josie asked, gazing down from atop Petunia.

I'll never be ready for this, Luke thought grimly, trying to ignore the way the fading sun set off lights in her hair, how the blue of her eyes put the sky to shame and how delectable her jeans-clad rump looked perched in that saddle. With a heavy sigh, he hauled himself onto the big-boned quarter horse.

Damn it all to Dallas, what was he doing, setting off on a moonlight trail ride with this woman? It was exactly what he'd sworn he wouldn't do.

It *would* be Manuel and Consuela's weekly square dance night. And the night Jack Ross had promised to have dinner with his in-laws. And Old Ben's poker night.

Sure seemed like everyone's social life was mighty active for a Monday evening, Luke thought suspiciously. Active enough that he smelled a rat. He'd bet dollars to donuts that Consuela's meddling hand was somehow behind this, but he knew he'd never be able to prove it. She'd been running behind-the-scenes interference in his life for as long as he could remember, and he'd never yet been able to catch her at it.

Well, she'd sure done a jam-up job on this little project, he thought with a black scowl. The only people who didn't have pressing engagements tonight were Butch and himself. The thought of spending an evening alone with Josie made him as nervous as a thief in church, but the thought of her alone in the moonlight with Butch had him reaching for a roll of antacids. He'd wasted no time concocting another errand for Butch.

"I don't see why you need me to take the truck in for a tune-up tonight," the ranch hand had grumbled, ogling Josie like a hungry wolf as she'd walked toward them on the path from the lodge to the corral. "I can take care of it just as easily in the morning."

"I'll need to use it in the morning," Luke had told him. "Can't afford to have it out of commission."

Butch had eyed him suspiciously. Luke had been able to tell the exact moment the light had clicked on in his brain. "Well, well, well! Now I get it." Butch had grinned slyly and nudged him with an elbow. "She's one fine-lookin' little filly. I admire your taste in women, boss."

Luke had opened his mouth to give a denial, then abruptly pressed his lips together. Josie was getting within earshot. Besides, if Butch thought he was interested in her, he'd leave her alone. Still, the whole idea of creating such a misconception left Luke uneasy.

Hell, everything about the situation left him uneasy, Luke thought now. Last night, for example. It bothered the heck out him that he'd had such a good time with her. They'd sat in the lodge kitchen for a couple of hours, talking about music and books and movies, about current events, global warming, even UFOs. He'd been surprised at how much they'd had in common, how smart and warm and funny she was. He'd had a wonderful time, and when he'd walked her back to her cabin, it had been tempting as all get-out to lean down and kiss her good-night.

He'd managed not to, but just barely. It was a good thing, too; the memory of that earlier kiss had been more than enough to make him toss and turn and curse a blue streak for most of the night. No telling what kind of state he would have been in if he'd kissed her again.

He was out of his mind, thinking about her in these terms, he told himself sternly. After what she'd told him about her family, he could almost believe she hadn't been in love with that jerk she'd nearly married, but that didn't mean she wasn't emotionally vulnerable, and the last thing he'd knowingly do was take advantage of a vulnerable woman.

Besides, he was determined to stick with women who understood ranch life, and Josie was so citified she probably wouldn't know a mosquito from a horsefly.

Even if she didn't have the first two strikes against her, Luke thought, the third one was more than enough to throw her out of the ball game completely: Josie was clearly the marrying kind. Since he had no intention of ever getting hitched again, that didn't leave much room for a relationship.

He looked up to find her watching him and felt a tug of attraction pull at his belly. Annoyed at the reaction, he shifted the reins to his right hand. "If you're all set, let's head on out."

"Don't we need to bring some supplies?"

"The food's in my saddlebag. Everything else is at the site. One of the ranch hands went out earlier and set things up."

"Sounds like you've got these cookouts down to a science."

Luke shrugged and nudged Black Star toward the gate of the corral. "They're a pretty popular activity."

Josie flicked her reins, and Petunia ambled beside him. "Do you serve as escort on many of them?"

"Not many." No point in telling her this was the first one he'd ever conducted for a guest. He didn't want her getting the idea he was giving her special treatment.

Because he wasn't, he thought stubbornly. He just didn't want Butch crawling all over her like an ant on a picnic blanket, that was all.

Butch swung the corral gate open, waved at Josie as she rode through, then gave Luke a broad wink behind her back. "Y'all have fun," he called.

Josie cast Luke a sidelong glance as she bounced along on Petunia on the trail through the meadow, confused and more than a little rattled at the thought of spending the entire evening alone with him.

She'd braced herself to deal with Butch. In fact, she had a whole speech prepared. No more hiding in the bushes for her, she'd decided firmly; she intended to confront the problem head-on. She'd planned to tell him she had no interest in any kind of romantic overtures, and if he persisted in making them, she'd consider it a form of harassment and take appropriate measures.

What those might be, she wasn't sure. Telling Luke, most likely.

But how the heck was she supposed to deal with *him?* Her feelings regarding any overtures he might make were a disturbingly different matter.

"If you don't usually handle the moonlight rides and cookouts, why are you pulling escort duty tonight?" she asked.

Luke's eyes narrowed. "Would you have preferred someone else?"

"No. I just wondered how it happened to be you."

His eyes were guarded. "All of the regular staff were busy."

"All of them?"

Luke's mouth tightened and a muscle flexed in his jaw. "Butch has an errand to run in town, if that's who you mean. Sorry to disappoint you." He urged his horse to a quicker pace and trotted ahead of her.

Josie stared after him, puzzled. Surely he couldn't think she was interested in Butch. Even if he had such a misguided notion, why would it put his nose out of joint? He couldn't be jealous.

Could he?

No. Still, the thought made her pulse quicken, and her thoughts again flew to that knee-melting, mind-bending kiss he'd given her yesterday. Both from his words and the strained silence that had followed, Luke had obviously regretted the impulsive act. There was no reason for her to think it would ever be repeated.

But she couldn't seem to get it out of her mind, and the memory of it somehow colored everything that had happened since. For something that had only lasted a few moments, Josie thought wryly, that kiss was sure taking up a lot of her time.

It had sat between them like a third party during the remainder of the tour yesterday, creating an awful awkwardness. And though the awkwardness had eased as they'd talked in the lodge kitchen last night, the tension had not. At least, not on her part. She'd been overly aware of his every move, his every glance, his every gesture.

She needed to put it out of her mind and just forget about it, she told herself. She was making entirely too much out of it, and it was causing her to overreact to every little thing he said or did.

Last night, for example. When he'd walked her back to her cabin along the darkened trail, her heart had pounded so hard she'd been sure he could hear it in the still, autumn night. At her door, her palms had gone damp, and something she thought she'd seen in his dark eyes had made her throat close up like a daylily at night. For long, vibrating seconds they'd just stood and looked at each other, and she'd been certain he was going to kiss her again.

Then he'd tipped his hat, bidden her good-night and turned on his heel to stalk off into the night. She'd watched him go, feeling as deflated as a punctured balloon, wondering why the sight of his retreating back should make her feel so let down and lonely.

Surely she hadn't *wanted* him to kiss her again, she'd reasoned with herself. It was too soon after her broken engagement. This was supposed to be her honeymoon, for heaven's sake! Why, it wasn't even decent to be thinking about kissing another man.

Yet she couldn't seem to think of anything else.

She looked at the rigid set of Luke's shoulders and realized she'd better think of something else fast if she didn't want to spend the evening in cold, miserable silence.

She prodded Petunia to catch up with his horse. "I only asked because I was curious about how you staff the ranch."

"Oh, really?" His voice was clearly skeptical.

"Yes. I hope to own a resort of my own someday, so I'm interested in how you manage things." Josie shifted her weight in the saddle, and Petunia snorted. Josie reached down and stroked the horse's neck.

Some of the wariness left Luke's eyes. "What kind of resort do you want to open?"

"Promise you won't make fun of me?"

"Depends. Does it have anything to do with cow chips?"

Josie laughed. "No. It has to do with families."

"You want to open a family resort?"

"Yes."

Luke gave a slow nod. "Our operation isn't set up for children, but we get a lot of inquiries. I think there's a real market for family destinations. What kind of place did you have in mind?"

"A casual place...kind of like a kid's summer camp. It would have activities the whole family could do together—swimming, horseback riding, crafts, canoeing, bicycling, cookouts, sing-alongs—those sorts of things."

Luke rubbed his jaw and regarded her thoughtfully. "You know, I think you're on to something. I bet a lot of folks would jump at the chance to do something like that. Sounds like a really good concept."

A warm cloud of pleasure enveloped her. She hadn't been sure her idea had any merit, although it was a dream she'd nurtured for a long time. She'd mentioned it once to her father, and he'd brushed it aside as a foolish daydream. She didn't know why she'd risked sharing it with Luke, or why his praise should give her such a deep-felt glow. His simple words had warmed her to the bone.

There was something solid and trustworthy about Luke. He was real and concrete, the kind of man who spoke bluntly, who wouldn't sugarcoat his words to fit what he thought someone wanted to hear. His opinions had weight and merit because he could be trusted to answer honestly. A person could put stock in what he had to say. And she admired and respected him for it in a way she'd rarely admired or respected anyone.

Certainly not anyone she'd ever kissed.

The thought made her stomach quiver. "Thanks. Of

course, at this point, that's all it is—a concept. I don't have the funds to open a place myself, and I don't yet have enough experience to approach any investors, but that's my long-term goal.''

"Long-term goals are good things to have."

"So what are yours?"

The question hung in the air for a moment, then Luke shook his head and gave a tight smile. "I have a feeling you won't approve."

"Why's that?"

"My goal is the exact opposite of yours."

"What do you mean?"

"Instead of building a resort, I'd like to shut one down."

"You mean you want to close the lodge?" she asked.

Luke nodded. "If I can ever get the ranch to the point where I no longer have to operate it, I want to tear the darn thing down and turn the site back into pastureland."

The reins went slack in her hand as she stared at him, and Petunia meandered so close to Black Star that Josie's leg brushed against Luke's. The brief physical contact shocked her almost as much as his remark. She jumped, inadvertently jerking Petunia to a stop. "You can't mean that."

The determined look on his face said otherwise. "I can. And I do."

"But why?" Josie nudged Petunia back into motion, taking care to keep a safe distance away from Luke.

"I never wanted the darn thing built in the first place."

Josie gazed at his taut mouth, his narrowed eyes, his stubbornly set chin and decided to brave the topic, anyway. "Consuela told me you argued with your dad over building it."

Luke cut a quick glance at her, then looked away. "Consuela talks too much."

"What happened, Luke?" Josie asked softly.

For a long moment she thought he wasn't going to reply. Then he shifted in his saddle and heaved a sigh. "The ranch went through a real rough spell a few years ago. Beef prices had fallen and profits were down. Dad and I had different ideas about how to handle it. I felt we needed to modernize our operation—to upgrade our facilities, improve our stock, expand our breeding program. But Dad thought we needed to diversify. He'd read an article that said tourism was the wave of the future, and he got it in his head that we should turn the Lazy O into a dude ranch."

"Did your father know anything about the hospitality industry?"

"Not a single thing. That was my biggest objection to the whole cock-eyed scheme." Luke's eyes burned with a dark intensity that made something tighten in Josie's stomach. "I've always believed in concentrating on one thing at a time—in sticking with what's tried-and-true and familiar, in developing specialties, in becoming really good at what you do."

There was no reason at all that his words should make her think of lovemaking, but her thoughts flew off on an erotic tangent all the same. She thought of Luke's face, concentrating as it lowered for a kiss; of his large, strong hands, becoming familiar; of the rest of his body, with its various specialties; and she had no doubt at all that he'd be really, really good—

Josie's face flooded with heat. She realized she'd been staring at his hands wrapped around the reins, taking in his long, tanned fingers, the masculine dusting of hair. She remembered how his hands had felt on her face and couldn't help but wonder how they'd feel other places. An illicit thrill chased through her at the thought. Abruptly she jerked her eyes back to his eyes and ordered herself to concentrate on his words.

"Besides, I was going through my divorce at the time and didn't want to deal with another big change right then. I'd acted rashly when I'd gotten married, and the last thing I wanted was to be involved in another rash mistake. I thought we should focus our resources on the ranch, not on opening a new business neither one of us knew anything about."

"Sounds like you had some valid reasons," she said.

Luke nodded. "But Dad wouldn't listen. When he got an idea in his head, he was like a pit bull with a porkchop—nothing could make him give it up." His mouth twisted in a mirthless smile. "He wasn't one to do anything halfway, either. He mortgaged the ranch for all it was worth and put all the money into constructing the lodge."

Luke ran a hand through his hair. "Dad said he would run the tourist part, and he wanted me to manage the ranch operation. But I didn't want to run a ranch that was nothing more than a sideshow for a bunch of tourists. I hated the thought of seeing the ranch I'd grown up working, that had been in our family for four generations, turned into some kind of Old West amusement park."

There was that sentimental side again. The realization made her feel strangely sentimental herself. "What happened?"

Luke gave a heavy sigh. "We argued, and I left."

"Where'd you go?"

"To manage a ranch in southwestern Oklahoma."

"Did you have any contact with your father while you were gone?"

"Oh, we exchanged a few letters and phone calls, but things were strained between us. He kept wanting me to come back, but I refused. I wouldn't even come for a visit.

I didn't want to see the lodge, didn't want to see how the ranch had changed. The thought of it just made me sick inside."

Given how deeply he loved the ranch, it was certainly understandable. A wave of sympathy washed through her. "Consuela said you came back when your dad became ill."

A nerve worked in Luke's jaw. "I headed straight here the moment she called." He stared ahead and was silent so long Josie didn't know if he was going to continue. Finally he blew out a harsh breath of air. "But it was too late."

"What do you mean?"

"He'd had a heart attack. He never regained consciousness."

"Oh, Luke—I'm so sorry."

"He'd worked himself to death, trying to operate both the ranch and the lodge. The ranch had gone through a real down cycle while I was away, but he didn't let anyone know how bad things were." Luke's voice was pained and bitter. He ran a hand down his face. "I never should have left. If I'd been here, I could have shouldered half the load for him, and maybe he would have taken better care of himself. Maybe I could have gotten him to a doctor sooner, when something could still be done."

Josie's heart turned over. "Surely you don't blame yourself for your father's death."

"Well, the way I see it, I *am* to blame." He briefly met her gaze, his eyes flat and pained. "And every time I manage to forget it for even a second, that blasted building is there to remind me."

He didn't hate the lodge because he disliked having guests on the ranch. He hated it because it reminded him of the argument. Guilt over not being there when his father needed him, not making peace with him before he died, was eating Luke alive.

The realization made something in Josie's chest twist and tighten. Luke was a man who cared deeply, who felt responsible for his actions, who had a strong sense of family obligation. She couldn't help but be struck by the difference between this man and the one she'd nearly married. Luke had a conscience. He had a sense of integrity. He had compassion and character. Robert had lacked all of those. How could she have failed to notice that fact? She'd been looking at all the wrong things.

She looked at Luke now, at his clenched lips and his rigid jaw, and knew he was angry at himself. A pang of sympathy, hot and acute, shot through her so sharply it hurt.

She searched her mind for a way to comfort him.

"Luke, you're being way too hard on yourself." She wished she weren't on horseback so she could reach out and touch him. "My guess is you were hurt that your father didn't take your feelings more into consideration. I know that's how I would have felt in your situation." Luke's eyes darted to her, then resumed staring straight at the pathway ahead. She couldn't tell what he was thinking, but at least he appeared to be listening. "You obviously loved your father a great deal or you wouldn't feel so bad about arguing with him. I don't think one person can love that strongly without the other person knowing it, Luke. Despite the disagreement, I'm sure he knew you loved him."

Her voice was earnest and persuasive. Luke looked at her, and their eyes locked and held. Josie's soft, soothing gaze poured over him like a balm. There was something healing in the concern that creased her brow, in the warmth of her sky-colored eyes. For a moment he almost let himself believe her words.

"I don't know about all that, but thanks for the thought."

She gave another soft smile, and he found himself staring at the way her lips curved upward. A hunger gnawed at his belly, a hunger that had nothing to do with a cookout and everything to do with her. He looked away, baffled at why she should have this odd effect on him. He could understand the physical attraction—that part was simple and straightforward. What he couldn't understand was why he was suddenly filled with these strong, strange longings for something deeper and more personal, and why he found himself talking a blue streak every time he got around her.

He was relieved when the trail narrowed at the edge of the woods. The single-file trail would make conversation difficult—which was a darn good thing, considering the fact that once again he'd spilled more guts than a filleted perch.

He reined in Black Star to let Josie precede him on the trail, wondering what on earth had gotten into him. He was normally the kind of man who kept his emotions under wraps, who played his cards close to his vest and didn't let the world know his business, yet here he'd gone again, telling her another sob story.

There was a lot more to her than was apparent on the surface. Not that there was anything wrong with her surface, he thought, eyeing her backside as she hypnotically swayed atop Petunia. No, siree, not anything at all.

He was grateful when they arrived at the campsite. He swung down from Black Star and tethered him to a tree, glad that it would be dark on the ride back. At least he'd be spared the torture of watching Josie rock back and forth in a saddle, he thought, turning to help her dismount from Petunia.

Her jacket rode up as he caught her around the waist, and the feel of her warm, naked skin sent shock waves pulsing through him. He froze, failing to step back and make room as her feet hit the ground. She lurched against his chest, her bottom gently bumping his groin. It was all he could do not to groan aloud.

She turned around in his arms. "Oh...sorry." Her breath felt whisper-soft on his face, and it smelled enticingly of cinnamon. Her eyes were mesmerizingly close. He'd never known the color blue could look so warm, he thought distractedly. He stared at her, his feet rooted to the ground like a heavy tree, afraid she'd bolt like a skittish colt if he made the slightest movement. Unwilling to risk it, he probably would have stood there, his hands on her waist, holding his breath, until he passed out.

He was spared that embarrassment when she stepped back and turned away. Luke grabbed Petunia's reins and haphazardly looped them around a tree limb, his pulse pounding as hard as the hooves of his best quarter horse at a full gallop.

He couldn't afford to have this reaction to her—especially not this early in the evening with the whole night stretching before them. He was here as a tour guide and host, nothing more.

He cleared his throat and gestured toward the clearing, where a circle of logs surrounded an enormous brick fire pit. Wood was already stacked in the center, just waiting to be touched with a match. "This is the campsite," he said unnecessarily.

Josie smoothed a strand of hair away from her forehead and turned toward it. "Looks like everything's all ready."

Oh, he was ready, all right. Ready to pull her back in his arms and run his hands through her thick, wild curls and kiss her halfway into tomorrow.

The thought made him scowl as he strode toward the campfire, squatted down and set it ablaze. Flames danced in the deepening dusk, adding extra sparks to a situation Luke was already finding unbearably overheated. How on earth was he going to make it through the evening without having a total meltdown?

* * *

The moon was full and high in the sky when Josie finally set her tin plate on the ground and gave a contented sigh. "That was one of the best meals I've ever eaten."

Luke placed his plate beside hers and leaned back against the log, gazing into the campfire. "Food always tastes better when it's cooked outdoors."

And when it's shared with good company, Josie thought, stretching her legs out in front of her. She'd been nervous about spending the evening alone with Luke—especially after she'd been all but immobilized with desire when he'd helped her down from her horse. The look in his eyes and the warmth of his hands on her skin had made her melt from the inside out, like a microwaved marshmallow.

Thank heavens things had lightened up as they'd grilled the steaks, roasted ears of corn and shared the salad Consuela had prepared. They'd shifted back into the easy, laughing rapport they'd shared in the kitchen the night before, and she almost felt relaxed.

Almost, but not quite. Attraction bubbled just beneath the surface, threatening to erupt like a volcano. Not knowing if or when it would add an underlying note of tension to the quiet surface of the evening.

She was attracted to a lot more than just Luke's physical appearance, and what he'd told her tonight about his argument with his father added fuel to the fire. She'd caught enough glimpses of the kind, caring man behind Luke's gruff exterior to want to see more.

She had no business feeling this way about him, she told herself sternly. For that matter, she had no business feeling *any* way about him. It was too soon after Robert to even think about another romantic entanglement.

So why could she seem to think of nothing else?

Luke suddenly sat up and pointed at the sky. "Look…a shooting star!"

Josie stared, enthralled, as a tiny speck streaked across the dark heaven and disappeared. "So that's what they look like!" she murmured.

Luke's eyebrows shot up. "You've never seen one before?"

"Afraid not."

He shook his head in amazement. "You city people are more deprived than I realized." His tone was teasing, but Josie sensed he meant every word. He leaned back against the log. "I used to make wishes on them when I was a boy. Mom said if you finished making your wish before the star disappeared, it would come true."

"That explains the shooting stars on your quilt," Josie said softly. No wonder it was so special to him, she thought. "What did you wish for when you were a boy?"

Luke gazed back up at the star-filled sky. "For everything to stay the same. I already had a pony and a dog and lots of toys, so I didn't waste wishes on those. And I never wanted to be an astronaut or a football player or a fireman—I always knew I wanted to stay right here and work the ranch when I grew up. So I used to just wish that nothing would change." He gave a short, humorless laugh. "'Course, I'd have stood a better chance if I'd wished for the Taj Majal to be air-dropped onto the south pasture." He looked at her. "What about you?"

Josie stared up at the twinkling sky. "I had two dreams. One was that summer camp would last all year long."

"You must have really liked it."

"I lived for it. It was just about my only chance to be outdoors."

"Why's that?"

Josie lifted her shoulders. "Not a lot of opportunity. My

family isn't the outdoorsy type. The only time my parents or sisters go outdoors is when they're getting in and out of a car—and that's only if they can't find covered parking.''

Josie grinned, but Luke had the feeling she wasn't exaggerating by much.

"But I loved the outdoors. When I grew too old to be a camper, I signed on as a counselor. That's when I discovered I loved working with people—especially people on vacation. It's what made me want to work in the hospitality industry." Josie looked away and sighed. "It probably wasn't the best basis for choosing a full-time career."

Luke's thoughts flew to what she'd told him earlier about her parents' disapproval of her career choice and her own doubts about her judgment. The discouraged tone of her voice stirred something protective inside him. "Hey, I think it's a great basis," he found himself saying. "You chose a career based on your interests and talents, and I think that shows excellent judgment."

Her eyes were searching and hopeful. "You really think so?"

"I do."

"As my father pointed out, I didn't take a lot of things into consideration—the long hours, the probability of living away from my family, the competition for advancement...."

"Every career has its drawbacks."

"But I ended up losing my job."

"That had nothing to do with your career choice. From what you told me, you were standing up for your principles. In my opinion, anyone who does that is not only exercising good judgment, but courage as well. Jobs are replaceable. Integrity is a different matter." The soft, grateful glow in her eyes made his heart do somersaults.

"Thanks," she murmured.

Luke nodded. Something that felt suspiciously like a knot was forming in his throat, and his chest had a spot that was decidedly tender. Unconsciously he rubbed it and tried to steer the conversation to a less emotionally laden topic. "You said you had two dreams. What was the other one?"

"Oh, the standard rose-covered cottage fantasy. To live in the country, have two or three children, a big dog and some horses."

The typical dream of an outdoor-starved city girl, Luke thought. If it ever came true, she'd be bored to tears in less than a week. "You left something important out of that bucolic little picture," Luke said dryly.

"What's that?"

"A husband. Ever do much dreaming about that?"

Josie gave a wry smile. "Based on the mistake I nearly made in that department, evidently not enough." She looked back up at the stars. "I always thought that when I met the right man, I'd know it."

He knew he was on dangerous ground, but he couldn't resist pushing the envelope. "How did you expect to know?"

"Oh, it sounds silly to say it aloud." She pulled up her knees and hugged them to her chest. "I guess I thought my heart would beat faster, that I'd feel all warm and alive whenever he was around, that deep inside I'd just know."

"Have you ever felt that way about a man?"

A log snapped on the fire, and sparks blazed into flame. It was dark, but not too dark to see a pink flush rise in her cheeks. "I've felt attraction before, if that's what you mean. But I'm sure that's all it was." She sounded breathless and oddly defensive, and her smile wobbled a little at the edge of her mouth.

Before he could figure out why she was acting so

strangely, she scrambled to her feet and dusted off her jeans. "It's getting late. We should probably be heading back, don't you think?"

In a more rational state of mind, he knew he would agree. But sitting beside her in the firelight had muddled his thoughts. Muttering agreement, Luke rose to dowse the fire and gather up the utensils, all the while wondering what type of man she was attracted to.

Wondering if she was attracted to him.

None of your damn business, he told himself. She's looking for a husband, not a playmate. All the same, thinking about the way she'd responded did funny things to his pulse rate and respiration, and he was glad when they'd finished securing the campsite. The sooner he put an end to this evening, the better.

The chorus of crickets reverberated loudly in the quiet night as they walked across the clearing toward the horses. The moon was round and full and so bright they didn't need to use the large-beamed flashlight Luke had brought— so bright, in fact, that even at a distance he could easily see only one horse standing where two had been tethered.

"Where's Petunia?" Josie asked.

Luke's heart sank heavily in his chest. "Back at the barn, most likely. I must not have tied her off well enough."

And he knew why, too, Luke thought darkly. He'd been so worked up over the feel of Josie's bare midriff he'd been unable to tie a simple knot.

Just thinking about it now sent another round of attraction ricocheting through him. He stalked toward the remaining horse in an effort to ward off the feeling, knowing all the while it was a lost cause.

"What are we going to do?"

"We'll both have to ride Black Star." He felt like a

doomed man discussing a trip to the gallows. "He balks at being led, and he's too skittish for you to ride him alone."

The prospect of riding the horse with Luke made Josie's mouth go dry. She managed a nod, and nervously waited as he shoved the flashlight and newspaper-wrapped dinnerware into the saddlebags. He swung into the saddle and reached down to help her up. Swallowing hard, Josie grabbed his arm, used the stirrup as a step and hoisted herself behind him.

She nearly slid off the other side. Luke's arm hooked back and caught her.

"Easy! You'll have to hold on tight."

"But there's nothing back here to hold on to."

"You'll have to hold on to me."

Her heart hammered against her ribs. Cautiously, hesitantly, she wrapped her arms around him. His denim jacket was open, and her hands landed on his stomach. It was flat and hard and warm, and the feel of it jarred her so much that she pulled away as if she'd been burned.

Oh, dear…exactly where was she supposed to grab hold? Maybe if she moved her hands up. Barely daring to breathe, she tentatively reached around him again.

This time her hands landed on his chest. She could feel his heart beating beneath her palm, and her own heart responded by pounding like a hailstorm. This was even worse than before. What on earth could she do now? She didn't dare move her hands down!

Black Star snorted and shied, and Josie clutched at Luke instinctively, flattening her breasts against him. He gave a sound like a grunt or a groan.

"Did I hurt you?" she gasped.

"No. I'm fine." He sounded anything but. His voice was thick and low and tense.

Josie's nose was pressed near the nape of his neck, and

as she drew a ragged breath, she inhaled the scent of his hair—a clean shampoo scent, mingled with a deeper, musky, manly essence. The scent made a curl of heat unfurl low in her belly. It occurred to her that his pillow must smell like this, and she was shocked to discover that her thoughts had ventured into his bedroom.

Conversation. That's what was needed to normalize this situation. "Is your house near here?" she asked.

"Why?" His voice was curt and wary.

Oh, mercy. Surely he didn't think she was suggesting— Josie swallowed. "I was just curious, that's all. You didn't show it to me when you showed me the rest of the ranch."

"It's not a part of the tour. I like to keep my privacy on at least one part of the ranch."

"Oh. Of course. I was only asking because Consuela told me your grandfather built it. I love old houses and—" Josie realized her voice had a strangled, panicked edge to it. "I was just curious, that's all," she finished lamely.

"Hey...it's okay." He adopted a gentler tone, as if he sensed her discomfort. "I wouldn't have minded showing it to you. I just didn't think of it. Especially not after..."

That kiss. His voice broke off, and the thought hung between them. Heat scorched her face and traveled lower, and she shifted on the horse, nearly losing her seat. Luke's arm again shot around and grabbed her. His hand landed at the top of her buttocks.

The pressure of his arm pulling her against his back nearly undid her. Oh, mercy, when was this ride going to be over? The smell of his hair, the feel of his chest, the beat of his heart—it was all too much to take. Her senses were on overload, her emotions ready to explode.

"Are you all right?" he asked.

No, her mind clamored fervently. "Yes," she responded weakly.

He released his grip and withdrew his arm. "Better hold on tight. You don't want to fall."

No, she didn't, she silently affirmed. Not off the horse. And even more certainly, not for him.

They rode in silence, the cedar-scented night pulsing around them. The very air seemed alive, filled with the throaty chirrups of tree frogs, the rhythmic clop of Black Star's hooves.

Finally the outline of the barn loomed ahead. By all rights she should have been relieved to see it, but for some perverse reason she was instead disappointed. Some traitorous, illogical part of her didn't want the ride to end, didn't want to relinquish the exquisite, disturbing, delicious sensation of holding Luke.

The thought made her hand shift on Luke's shirtfront, her fingers splaying across his chest. She heard his breath catch in his throat.

Hers did the same when his hand rose and covered hers. It was a simple gesture—his warm, large hand capturing hers against his heart—yet it struck Josie as terrifyingly, thrillingly profound, filled with meaning and fraught with peril.

She should move, she should pull away, she should just lift her hand.

She should, but she didn't.

Was she entering into some kind of tacit agreement by remaining so still? She didn't know. All she knew was that she didn't want the moment to end.

Black Star abruptly stopped. Josie peered around Luke's shoulder and saw that they'd arrived at the corral.

"Well, here we are," Luke said. "I'll help you down as soon as I tether Black Star to the fence."

He somehow managed to swing off the horse without dislodging her.

The next thing she knew, he was reaching up to help her down—and then she was in his arms, her body sliding against his in heart-stopping slow motion as she slipped off the horse.

Her feet met the ground, and her gaze met his. The light in his eyes sparked something deep within her, like a match to dry hay. They stood eye to eye, chest to chest, belly to belly, her arms wound around his neck. She'd been thinking about kissing him for so long that it seemed like the most natural thing in the world to tug his head down until his lips touched hers.

The kiss started out slow and gentle, then rapidly gained momentum, feeding on itself like a forest fire. It went beyond attraction. It soared into the realm of passion—wild, fierce, hungry, white-hot passion. He tightened his arm around her, and she fitted herself against him, seeking to get close, then closer still.

He unlocked something deep within her, something previously untouched—some deep, hidden part that needed to be understood and accepted and believed in. Why this should be so, why he should be the one to make her feel this way, why she should respond to him so intensely baffled her nearly as much as how she could be melting into a puddle of emotion and desire and longing, fast reaching a point of no return.

No return. The thought jarred her. She couldn't let herself just get swept away. She needed to exercise some judgment, some control over her own destiny. She'd let herself be swept along on a tide of events once before, and she'd vowed she'd never surrender control of her life again.

His hand slid up her waist, his fingers on her back, his thumb on her ribs—up, up, up until his thumb curved under her breast, then higher to strum across the tip. Her knees weakened, and so did her resolve. Oh, mercy—another few moments of this and all of her good intentions would be forgotten.

With an effort she pulled away. "I...I need to go," she gasped. Turning, she fled down the path toward her cabin.

Luke watched her go, struggling with his own raging emotions. He propped both of his hands against the rail fence and drew a deep, steadying breath.

Dammit, it was just what he'd sworn wouldn't happen. Just exactly what he'd feared.

Being alone with Josie and trying to keep his hands off her was like laying a bed of catnip before a kitten and saying, "Don't roll in it." It was like holding an apple to Black Star's muzzle and saying, "Don't take a bite." It was like tossing a bale of hay to a half-starved bull and expecting it to still be there half an hour later. She was an irresistible temptation, and he'd known better than to get himself into a situation where he was alone with her.

Dammit! He'd nearly succeeded in making it through the evening. But then he'd gotten one taste of her soft, sweet lips and all bets were off.

Five more days, he thought grimly. Just five more days, and she'd be off the ranch and out of his life. Then maybe, just maybe, he could sleep through the night, focus on his work and think about something other than the sound of her laugh, the scent of her skin and those haunting, heart-breakingly blue eyes.

Chapter Seven

A shrill whistle echoed through the lodge, causing Luke to freeze in his tracks in the middle of the main hall.

What in deuces was that? Whatever it was, it sounded like it came from the guest room quarters. With a muttered oath, Luke clutched the employee time sheets he'd come to collect and headed off to investigate.

He found Consuela standing in the hallway outside an open guest room door.

"What's going on?" he asked, craning his neck to peer inside. He stared in surprise as two pudgy, middle-aged chambermaids raced around the room's two beds, smoothing and tucking the sheets, jamming pillows into pillow cases and yanking up the bedspreads in record time. In the six months he'd known these women, he'd never seen them move faster than slugs. Come to think of it, they usually looked about as neat as slugs, too. Yet here they were, sporting brand-new black-and-white maid uniforms and looking as dapper as a pair of penguins.

"It's a bed-making race," Consuela said. "Isn't it exciting?"

Thrilling. And he bet he could just guess who was behind all the excitement, he thought with a scowl. His eyes scanned the room for Josie. Sure enough, there she was, standing in the corner, her eyes riveted on a stopwatch, her hair curling about her shoulders in wild abandon. His stomach tightened at the sight of her, and the unwelcome reaction only increased his annoyance.

He'd managed to avoid her for the past three days, but he hadn't managed to get her off his mind. It didn't help matters that Consuela and Manuel couldn't stop talking about her. Josie had done this, Josie had done that, Josie had recommended so and so. They prattled on so about her, you'd think she'd hung the moon.

Josie had evidently helped Consuela select and train two new employees, and she'd instituted some kind of incentive program to encourage the housekeeping staff to show up on time and improve their job performance. And while Luke had to admit the lodge was running more smoothly, her involvement in the operation of the place bothered him no end.

She'd started out peeling potatoes, and now she was darn near running the whole show. It just wasn't right. She was a paying guest, by golly, and she had no business being so involved in the operation of the lodge. The whole situation made him flat-out uneasy.

One of the maids plopped a mint on a pillow and threw her hands up in the air. "All done!" she shouted.

The second maid quickly followed suit. "Me, too!"

Josie clicked the stopwatch and beamed at the maids. "That was terrific, ladies. You beat your old time by ten full seconds. Shave off another ten seconds next time, and

Consuela will give you each a pound of coffee to take home.''

"Great!" The taller of the two maids turned to her co-worker. "You know, Myra, that was a lot of fun."

"Yeah. Didn't seem like work at all," agreed the other.

"I think work *should* be fun," Josie said. "We'll have another race later in the week. In the meantime, you can practice improving your time every time you make a bed. And remember—if you both report to work on time all week, clean all your allotted rooms during your shifts and complete all the tasks on your checklists, you'll win a take-home family dinner on Friday."

The maids smiled broadly. "I can't wait. It'll be awfully nice to skip cookin' for an evenin'," Myra said.

"You're not kiddin'," agreed the other. "I can use every break I can get."

"I'm sure you'll both be getting a break on Friday." Josie gave each of them a warm pat on the shoulder. "It's a team effort, though. Both of you have to meet the goal."

"We won't let each other down," said the taller one solemnly. "Right, Myra?"

Myra nodded vigorously. "Right."

With a broad smile, Josie stepped out of the room, into the hall and smack into Luke's chest.

"Oh!" Her eyes flew wide.

Their startling blue color struck him like a bucket of cold water. He grabbed her by the shoulders, intending to steady her, but he suddenly didn't feel any too steady himself. Her soft, feminine scent teased his nostrils and played havoc with his composure.

He hid it under a scowl. "What the heck is going on here?" he asked gruffly. "And just who authorized all this, anyway?"

Consuela stepped up and stretched her round form to its

full four feet ten inches. "I did. If you have any questions, you can talk to me."

Luke stepped back and rubbed his chin. Heck, he'd always let Consuela handle everything concerning the lodge's domestic staff. He trusted her judgment in these matters more than his own. But it galled him to think that she was blindly following Josie's suggestions.

"What are they doing in uniforms?"

"It gives them a sense of identity and helps build team spirit," Josie piped up. "And it looks a lot more professional from your guests' standpoint."

"Hmm." He didn't like it, but he couldn't say exactly why. "What are these checklists they were talking about?"

"Oh, those are *¡muy bueno!*" Consuela raved. "Josie made a list of all the chores that have to be done for the rooms to pass the mustard."

Luke furrowed his brow. "For the rooms to *what?*"

"Pass muster." Josie flashed her dimple. "The checklist gives Consuela an objective set of criteria for evaluating their work and lets the maids know exactly what's expected of them. When they meet or exceed their job requirements, they earn incentive prizes."

"And it's working wonders," Consuela said, clutching her hands together ecstatically. "Josie's done the same thing for the kitchen staff. I don't know why I never thought of this myself."

Luke's brow darkened. "Probably because you have more sense than to start giving away the ranch."

Consuela shook her head. "We're only giving things we buy in bulk or have to prepare, anyway." She wagged a finger at Luke. "Believe me, it's not nearly as expensive as advertising and training new employees every other week."

Luke frowned down at his boots. Everything they said

made perfect sense. Regardless of the source of the ideas, they were good ones. Why did it bother him so that Josie happened to be the one to initiate them?

Because she was a guest, he thought stubbornly. It wasn't seemly and it wasn't her place.

But there was more to it than that. The fact of the matter was he didn't want to be beholden to her. He didn't want to need her, and he darn sure didn't want to miss her when she was gone.

The thought made him squirm in his boots. He needed to get her out of the lodge and back into vacation mode, and he needed to do it fast.

He glanced at her. "Your overnight canoe trip's scheduled for tomorrow. I'll set it up for Manuel to be your canoe partner, and Consuela can join the two of you for the camp out."

"Oh, I can't be away from the lodge that long," Consuela demurred, waving her hand. "I have to supervise the cleanup after dinner and breakfast in the morning."

"Nonsense. From what you've told me, your kitchen help is showing up on time and you've got everything more under control than ever." Luke gave her a coercive smile. "I'll drop you off at the campsite late in the afternoon when I take the supplies, then I'll pick you up first thing in the morning."

Consuela frowned. Luke could practically see the wheels turning in her head. She'd been none too subtle about trying to match him up with Josie, and she probably didn't want them separated for most of Josie's remaining time. Her eyes suddenly lit up. "I have a wonderful idea! You should take her, Luke. You haven't been on a camp out in years."

He hadn't expected a suggestion this blatant even from Consuela. He narrowed his eyes. "I'm sure Josie will be much more comfortable with another woman along."

"I don't want to create any extra work for Consuela," Josie said worriedly. "Maybe we should just skip the whole thing."

"I won't hear of it," Luke said firmly. "It's part of your package. Besides, Consuela and Manuel love camping out. Why, Manuel told me they went camping at Lake Tenkiller just last weekend. And the weather should be great. This warm spell is supposed to last through the weekend."

"I really don't mind going by myself," Josie said.

Luke shook his head. "Our insurance doesn't allow it. Besides, I'm sure Consuela and Manuel will be more than happy to escort you." Luke gave Consuela a meaningful look, then turned and stalked down the hall.

That should keep Josie out of his hair for a couple of days, he thought with satisfaction. With Consuela and Manuel watching her, she was sure to stay out of trouble. And with her off the ranch and out of reach, hopefully he could stay out of trouble, too.

"The campsite's just around this bend," Manuel called from the rear of the canoe. "I bet Luke and Consuela are already there."

Josie peered ahead as the craft floated around the curve of the river, her pulse unaccountably picking up speed. Sure enough, there they were, setting up a camp in a clearing in the distance.

Consuela was closer to the shore, in plain view as she pulled a large black skillet from a box of cooking supplies, but it was the familiar figure behind her that caught and held Josie's full attention.

Luke. Her eyes hungrily drank in the sight of him, noting every detail of his appearance—the way his dark hair looked like he'd just combed it with his fingers, the breadth of his shoulders in his blue flannel shirt, how his thigh muscles bunched against his jeans as he crouched down to arrange wood on a campfire. The blood suddenly seemed to run hotter and faster through her veins.

Not counting the conversation in the lodge hallway yesterday, she hadn't seen him since the trail ride. She was certain he'd been avoiding her, and she was equally certain it was because of that kiss.

He sure hadn't minded kissing her at the time, she thought. She might have initiated it, but he'd been a more-than-willing participant. She grew warm just thinking about the way his lips had seared a trail of pleasure across her mouth and throat while his hands had roamed her body.

Whatever his reasons, she told herself, she should be relieved he'd been keeping his distance. Romance was the last thing she needed at this point in her life, and not seeing Luke meant not having to deal with the confusing, distracting, disturbing feelings he aroused in her.

All the same, a secret, less sensible part of her had been on the constant lookout for him. At night, the memory of his kisses had burned in her mind, making her toss and turn until the sheets were snarled and the covers were twisted. She knew her behavior was illogical, but knowing that only increased her sense of irritation and frustration.

Luke looked up and met her gaze. Even at this distance, she felt blistered by a burst of attraction. Determined not to show it, she raised her hand and waved. He straightened and waved back, then headed to the shore to meet them.

The bottom of the canoe scraped loudly on the small, smooth rocks as Manuel grounded the craft. Luke stretched out a hand and helped Josie climb out. His grip was warm and strong, and the feel of it sent an unwanted thrill chasing up her arm. She deliberately avoided his eyes, not wanting him to see the effect his touch was having on her.

"Did you have a good trip?" he asked.

"Wonderful. The fall foliage is just incredible." She held up the camera hanging around her neck. "I shot two rolls of film."

Luke smiled. "The trees really put on a show this time of year. Autumn has always been my favorite time for float trips."

Josie swallowed, trying to compensate for her suddenly dry mouth, and tried to ignore the fact that Manuel was greeting Consuela with an enthusiastic kiss. The last thing she wanted to think about right now was kissing. "Do you go canoeing often?" she asked.

He shook his head. "I haven't set foot in one in years. With the lodge and the ranch, I've been too busy to take any time off."

"It's a shame to live in a place this beautiful and not take time to enjoy it."

Luke shrugged. "I can hardly take time to sleep until I find a manager for the lodge."

"Any prospects?"

"I interviewed an applicant this morning, but Consuela didn't care for him."

Consuela gave a derisive snort. "He was a real low light."

Josie's brow creased. "A what?"

"She means a low-life," Luke translated, grinning.

"He was bossy and conceited and rude," Consuela said with a sniff.

"Besides that, his references didn't check out." Luke shoved his hands in his pocket and shifted his stance, as if he was anxious to get moving. "It's getting late, and we need to set up camp before dark. Manuel, why don't you go see if you can find some more firewood."

The man nodded. "Sure thing, boss."

"And I'll go get the rest of the food out of the Jeep," Consuela said.

"I'll get that for you, Consuela," Luke volunteered.

Consuela waved her hand and shook her head. "There's just one little bag left—I can manage fine. You stay here with Josie." She gave Luke a meaningful look. "You've hardly seen her at all the past few days. I'm sure you'd like a chance to thank her for all her help at the lodge."

Josie watched Consuela traipse up the embankment, her face burning at the woman's obvious ploy to leave them alone.

Luke cleared his throat and looked at her. His Adam's apple bobbed as he swallowed. "She's right. I've been meaning to tell you how much I appreciate all of your assistance."

"I've enjoyed helping out."

"There's another thing I've been meaning to say." His Adam's apple jerked again. "I, uh, want to apologize for the other night."

Josie's palms grew damp. He could only mean one thing—but why was he apologizing? She was the one who'd initiated that kiss. "That's not necessary." She stared down at the ground, pretending to raptly study a leaf. "It was just one of those things."

He gave a curt nod and absently kicked a stone with his toe. "Well, I've felt bad about it."

He felt bad about kissing her? What a flattering remark! Her spine stiffened and her voice took on a chill. "No need. If anyone should be apologizing, it's me."

"No, I take full responsibility. I didn't mean to take advantage of you."

"Take advantage of me?" she asked incredulously. Exactly what did he mean by *that*? Why, it almost sounded as if he thought she was some feeble-brained incompetent who couldn't look out for herself. Even more galling, the remark implied he wielded some kind of power over her.

She fixed him with her frostiest stare. "Whatever makes you think you could do that?"

Luke shrugged. "Well, you're here on a honeymoon alone and all, and I know how vulnerable a person can be when they're on the rebound."

"Hold it right there." Josie held up a hand. "Are you implying I don't know my own mind?"

"I'm not implying anything. I'm just saying that under the circumstances, you might be more receptive to a man's advances than usual, that's all."

Josie planted her hands on her hips and glared at him. "Why would you think a thing like that?"

Luke shrugged. "Well, when you decided to come to the Lazy O, you thought you were going to be a newlywed. It's only natural that you'd be expecting to have a certain set of...experiences while you were here. And since you had those expectations, you're probably more vulnerable to someone who could, well, potentially meet those expectations."

Josie gazed at him hotly. "Thank you for that extremely flattering analysis, Dr. Freud! I wasn't aware that psychiatry was one of your specialties, but—"

A loud wail rent the air, causing Josie to break off in mid-sentence. "What's that?"

"Ooooohhh! Oww-eee!" The distinctly human moan came from the embankment above.

"Consuela!" Manuel gasped. The wiry man raced from the woods, dropping logs as he ran, and scrambled up the embankment like a man half his age.

Luke charged after him, his heart in his throat. Consuela was the closest thing he had to family, and he loved the feisty woman like a second mother. He was vaguely aware that Josie followed closely behind.

He and Manuel arrived simultaneously to find Consuela on the ground beside the Jeep, clutching her ankle.

"Is it a snakebite?" Luke demanded.

Manuel spoke to Consuela in rapid Spanish, then glanced up at Luke. "No. She says she twisted her ankle."

"Oohh," Consuela moaned again.

Josie peered over his shoulder. "Do we have any ice?"

Good idea. The thought registered in Luke's mind through a haze of worry. "In the Jeep," he replied.

Josie rapidly climbed in, located the ice chest and wrapped some ice in a paper towel.

"Here," she said, climbing back down and handing the makeshift ice pack to the housekeeper.

"*Gracias.*" Consuela placed it above her foot, moaning again.

"It's the same ankle she fractured last spring," Manuel said worriedly.

"Can you stand?" Luke asked.

"I don't know. It hurts too bad to try."

"She probably shouldn't put any weight on it until it's checked by a doctor," Josie said quickly. "Especially if it was recently injured."

Luke glanced at her. "You're right. Manuel, you need to take her into town and get it X-rayed." Luke dug in his pocket and extracted a set of keys. "Take the Jeep."

"But what about the camp out?" Consuela moaned.

"Don't worry about it. I'll take care of everything."

"We don't have to stay," Josie protested. "Maybe they could drop us off at the lodge."

"The Jeep's a two-seater," Luke said curtly. "There's no room. We'll be fine here."

Was it his imagination, or did a ghost of a smile cross

Consuela's lips? An unthinkable consideration crossed Luke's mind, making him frown.

Nah. He felt disloyal to even think it. Consuela was an incorrigible matchmaker, but surely she wouldn't go so far as to fake an injury just to get him alone with Josie.

Would she?

Luke's gaze swept to Manuel, and the expression on the older man's face made him put his misgivings aside. Manuel's face was ashen, his forehead creased with worry. One thing was for sure—if Consuela was faking it, she hadn't let her husband in on the stunt.

With an effort, Manuel and Luke lifted Consuela into the Jeep. Manuel hurried around to the driver's seat.

"If her injury's not too serious, Manuel, perhaps—" Luke stopped in mid-sentence. What was he going to do— ask Manuel to abandon his injured wife and come back later just so he wouldn't end up alone with Josie? He couldn't bring himself to do that. And he couldn't ask Manuel to call in another ranch hand, either. At this hour, they were all home with their families.

For heaven's sake, Josie and he were both mature adults, he thought with irritation. Surely they could make it through a single evening without a chaperon. "Never mind. You just take care of Consuela. You can send someone to get us first thing in the morning."

Manuel nodded. Luke grabbed the ice chest and a remaining bag of groceries from behind the seat, then watched as the ranch hand climbed in and drove away.

Josie stood beside him as the taillights disappeared. He heard her give a ragged sigh. "Poor Consuela," she murmured. "I feel so badly for her."

"Me, too. I hope she didn't break that ankle again."

"Manuel looked so worried," Josie said pensively. "He almost seemed in worse shape than Consuela."

"He probably is. He adores her."

"She feels the same way about him. They're lucky to have each other."

It was a simple statement, but standing there with her on the edge of twilight, it seemed loaded with disturbingly personal implications. It made Luke all too aware of the voids in his own life and caused a heavy, aching emptiness to gnaw inside him.

The sun was fast sinking behind the trees, its fading light painting the clouds misty shades of pink and orange and purple. Luke gestured toward the trail.

"Come on, it's getting dark. If we want to avoid any more injuries, we'd better set up camp while there's still light."

Josie nodded and followed him down the trail. They walked together in silence, but the harsh words they'd exchanged before the accident resounded in his mind. If he was going to make it through this evening, he needed to smooth things over. "Josie..." he began.

"Luke..." she said at the exact same moment.

They both froze and looked at each other. "Go ahead," she prompted.

"Ladies first."

"I'd rather hear what you were going to say."

Luke ran a hand through his hair and blew out a harsh breath of air. "If I somehow offended you earlier, I'm sorry. I was just trying to apologize for the other night." He swallowed and looked directly at her. "I know this situation is darned awkward. I just want you to know you don't have to worry about...about—" He swallowed again. "—about anything. I mean, nothing is going to happen."

A flash of irritation snapped in her eyes. "You're darned right, it's not."

Jeez, she didn't have to make it sound as if it was such

a distasteful concept, did she? Last time he looked, he hadn't sprouted horns or a second head.

And she *had* kissed him. Twice.

"Well, fine." Luke set about picking up the logs Manuel had scattered, his feelings strangely injured by the vehemence of her response. "I just wanted to set your mind at ease, that's all."

"It's perfectly at ease," she retorted.

Luke straightened and looked at her. The last rays of sunset were casting some kind of soft pink light on her, making her skin look as sun kissed and delicious as a ripe peach. Her hair was backlit into a fiery halo, and light streamed through the loose weave of her cotton sweater, revealing the curves hiding underneath. He felt an absurd urge to grab her in his arms, bend her backward and kiss her until they were both breathless and dizzy and too aroused to think.

Instead he swallowed hard, averted his eyes and nodded. "Well, good. I'm glad that's settled."

But it wasn't settled. Not at all, Josie thought as she looked at him later in the glow of the campfire. The conversation had drifted to other topics as they'd built the fire, set up the tent and cooked their dinner, but attraction swirled around and between them like autumn leaves in the evening wind. Despite her bold words, the possibilities of the evening smoldered like the embers in the campfire.

The temperature was dropping. Josie huddled close to the dying fire, her arms wrapped around her knees. "I wonder how Consuela is doing," she mused aloud.

"She's probably full of medication and in no pain at all. Most likely Manuel is in worse shape than she is."

Josie looked up and smiled, but when she turned her gaze back to the fire, her face grew solemn. "I've always admired couples with the kind of love they seem to have. My best friend's parents had that kind of close relationship, and I always wanted a marriage like that someday.''

''Your own parents' marriage isn't like that?''

Josie shook her head. ''They get along fine, but they have entirely separate lives. Don't get me wrong—they're happy enough, so I guess it suits them. But they're not close-knit like Manuel and Consuela.'' Josie gazed at Luke. He was seated beside her, cross-legged, facing the fire. ''What about your folks?''

Luke stretched out his legs and leaned back on his elbows. ''They were inseparable.''

''It must have been rough on your dad when your mom died,'' she said softly. ''Was it sudden?''

Luke nodded. ''A car crash.''

''How awful! Was she alone?''

''No.'' Luke's profile flickered into shadows as a gust of wind temporarily dimmed the fire. A second later the flames leapt high, starkly illuminating the grim set of his mouth and the lines of pain around his eyes. ''I was with her.''

''Oh, Luke.'' His name came out as a whisper. Josie's hand flew to her mouth, her heart turning over. ''What happened?''

A nerve worked in his jaw as he stared into the fire. ''It was a Saturday afternoon, and we were driving home after a Little League game in town. Dad had stayed at the ranch because a mare had injured a leg and a vet was coming to look at it. I was eager to get home and tell Dad all about the game—I'd fielded a two-base hit and my team had won, and Mom had taken me for ice cream afterward to celebrate. All of a sudden a dog wandered onto the highway. Mom swerved to miss it, and the next thing I knew, the car was rolling down a hill. I woke up in the hospital with a concussion, two broken ribs and a broken arm.'' He fell silent. An owl hooted in the distance. ''But none of that hurt anywhere near as much as getting the news I'd lost my mom.''

Josie sat motionless, sympathy flowing through her. She wished with all her heart she could somehow transfuse it into Luke, somehow ease the pain she heard in his voice. Not knowing what else to do, she silently stretched out her hand.

He covered it with his own. Her fingers felt warm and small and somehow right in his palm. He glanced over at her and was shocked to discover that her eyes were full of tears.

No one had cried for him in a long, long time. Not in years. Heck, as far as he knew, probably not since all this had happened.

He gazed at Josie, moved beyond words that she was crying for him now, and a cold, hard place inside of him began to crack and thaw. He didn't know why she cared so much, but the fact that she did somehow soothed the old, aching scars on his heart.

Warm, tender, unnamed emotions bubbled up inside of him, flooding his chest, choking his throat, making his heart thud painfully against his ribs.

She turned her face away so that her hair hid her features, and wiped her eyes with the back of her free hand. She clearly didn't want him to see her tears, but he couldn't pull his eyes away.

''That must have been so hard for you,'' she said at length.

He gazed at her, not knowing how to deal with the strange emotions pulsing through him, not knowing what to do at all. She'd awakened something inside of him, something that hadn't stirred in years, and now it was yawning and stretching and fluttering to life. For lack of a better plan, he decided to simply keep talking.

He nodded. "It was hard on Dad, too. After the funeral he wouldn't leave his study for a full week. Manuel finally went in and somehow talked him into coming out." Luke looked off in the distance. "In a lot of ways, though, it seems like Dad never did come out. I'd see him at mealtime, and that was about it. I used to think he blamed me for Mom's death. I used to think that if he did, he was probably right. If I hadn't wanted to play baseball, we wouldn't have been driving back from town. If I hadn't fielded that hit, we wouldn't have stopped for ice cream...."

"Oh, Luke. You don't still think that, do you?"

Luke shook his head. "No. And I don't believe Dad ever consciously did, either. But things were always distant between us after Mom died. I tried and tried to draw him out, to get involved in his life or get him involved with mine, but there was always a wall between us. I felt like I was a disappointment to him. I felt like nothing I could ever do or say or be could make up for what happened. He just didn't seem interested in spending time with me, in getting to know what I thought or felt. When he insisted on building the lodge over my objections, that was the final straw. I realized I was probably never going to measure up in his eyes, and I might as well stop trying."

"It must have been so lonely for you," Josie said, her voice so low it was almost a whisper. "You not only lost your mother, but your father, as well."

How did she know? Intuitively, she'd zeroed in on his deepest wound.

Suddenly he knew why he opened up to her so easily, why he talked to her with such abandon. *She listened with her heart.* She not only tried to understand, but to feel what he was feeling. It was a rare and special gift, the way she listened. Especially to someone who'd felt shut out and disconnected for as much of his life as he had.

Luke tightened his grip on her hand, savoring the feel of her fingers twined with his.

"It was lonely, all right. And I promised myself I'd never do that to someone I loved—that if a friend or relative ever needed me, I'd be there for them." Luke's sigh was long and deep. "But when Dad needed me most, I wasn't there for him, either." Gazing into the flames, he shook his head in self-disgust. "Like father, like son, huh?"

He felt the pressure of her fingers inside his hand. "You didn't do it deliberately. And I'm sure your dad didn't deliberately withdraw from you, either. Grief can make people do funny things."

So can moonlight, Luke thought. What was the matter with him, running his jaw like an outboard motor? "Hey, I didn't mean to burden you with all this. This is your vacation, for Pete's sake. Let's talk about something more pleasant."

"I don't feel burdened. I feel—" Josie stopped abruptly. Oh, mercy, what she was going to say? *Connected? Close to you?* Those would never do. *Moved? Touched?* He'd probably think she was touched in the head.

"Like I'm getting to know you," she finished lamely.

He looked at her, his eyes as warm and dark as black coffee, and something in his gaze sent a hot shiver racing through her. Another apt word flashed in her mind: *attracted.*

Judging from the smoldering light in his eyes, she didn't need to say it aloud. He was reading it, loud and clear…and sending the same message back.

Her cheeks flooded with heat. She grew acutely aware

that he was still holding her hand, and her breath caught in her throat as he began tracing a finger across her wrist.

"I feel like I'm getting to know you, too," he said in a low, husky voice, leaning close enough that she could feel his breath on her face.

The air between them grew electrified. The rush of the river, the crackle of the fire, the rustle of the leaves in the wind, the bite of autumn chill in the air intensified almost unbearably. Then he lifted her hand to his mouth, and her awareness of all other sensations receded.

His lips gently grazed the back of her hand. Her joints went limp, and her thoughts grew fuzzy and her heart thrummed as fast as a hummingbird's wings. Slowly he rotated her wrist and planted a soft kiss on her pulse point, then brushed her palm with his lips. Her fingertips curled against his face, rasping against the late-day stubble of his cheek.

Never had she dreamed her hand was such an erogenous zone. The sensation of his lips against it was so devastatingly restrained, so exquisitely tender that it made her shiver.

He felt her fingers tremble against his face, and an answering tremor reverberated through him. Never had he wanted a woman as he wanted Josie now. He wanted to pull her into his arms, to trace the features of her face with his lips, to stroke her hair, to bury his nose in her neck and inhale her scent, to kiss her into oblivion, then come up for air and start all over again. He wanted to undress her, to caress every inch of her body, to give her slow, excruciating pleasure, to love her in all the ways that a man could love a woman—

Love her? Where the heck had that thought come from?

And what the hell was he doing, anyway? He'd promised her that nothing would happen. She was a guest at the lodge, for Pete's sake—a guest who'd shelled out good money for this camp out, who had every right to expect he wouldn't use it as an opportunity to seduce her. Even if she were more than willing, he couldn't in good conscience take advantage of a woman in her emotionally vulnerable circumstances.

He abruptly dropped her hand. "It's getting late. We should probably try to get some shut-eye." He pushed himself to his feet, strode into the shadows and returned with two sleeping bags. "You take the tent, and I'll sleep on the other side of the campfire near the river."

He had no idea if she intended to sleep in her clothes or change into nightclothes, but the thought of her getting ready for bed made his mouth dry. He thrust a sleeping bag at her. "Here. I'll go for a walk and give you some privacy. Good night."

He turned on his heel and stalked off into the night before he had a chance to think any further. Every thought he formed was more disturbing that the preceding one, and if he didn't hightail it away from her now, he might just invent a few reasons to stay.

It was cold. Teeth-chattering, bone-freezing, toe-aching cold.

I've never felt so cold in my life, Josie thought as she shivered inside the sleeping bag. She was almost too cold to move. She haltingly raised an arm and checked the green luminescent dial of her watch for the fifth time in the past hour. Not quite three. Oh, mercy, at least three more hours until dawn, and they were sure to be the coldest hours yet.

She couldn't just lie here and freeze to death. She had to do something. Maybe she could get warm beside the campfire.

Shaking like a shorn lamb in a snowstorm, she wrapped

the sleeping bag around her and crawled out of the small dome-shaped tent.

The campfire was extinguished. Her heart sank as the wind howled around her, slicing right through her.

"Are you all right?"

She turned and saw Luke propped against a tree, huddled inside his sleeping bag. Clutching her own bag as tightly about her as she could, she walked toward him. "I'm fr-freezing. I thought I could g-g-get warm by the fire, but it's g-g-gone out."

"It's too windy for a campfire. Can't risk burning down the forest." Luke glanced up at the sky, and Josie followed his gaze. Clouds scudding across the moon, obliterating most of the stars. "This must be that cold front that the weather forecaster swore would miss us."

"D-do you happen to have any extra blankets? I'm wearing every p-piece of c-c-clothing I brought, but I'm so c-c-cold my feet hurt."

Luke unzipped his sleeping bag and climbed out. "Here," he said, extending the bag to her. "Take mine."

"Oh, n-no. You'll freeze!"

He gave a shrug. "I'll be okay."

Josie gazed at him in the moonlight. His flannel shirt, jeans and denim jacket were no match for the wintry blasts of wind stripping the oaks of their autumn glory. He was trying to act nonchalant, but she could tell his teeth were chattering. She shook her head and handed back the sleeping bag. "This is no time for g-gallantry."

"Then we've only got one option. We'll have to zip the bags together and share our body heat."

Josie's stomach fluttered at the thought. Given the undeniable attraction between them, they were playing with fire to crawl into a sleeping bag together.

But right now she was so miserably cold she'd welcome

any kind of fire she could get. A shiver seized her, shaking her so hard she almost lost her grip on the sleeping bag she was clutching. She managed an awkward nod.

"Let's go to the tent. It'll at least shield us from the wind," he said.

Josie hurried toward it and ducked through the flap. The muffled whine of the wind through the nylon fabric seemed almost quiet after the noisy bluster outside.

The tent was small, and when Luke stepped inside, it seemed even smaller. Just his presence in the intimate space seemed to warm it a degree or two.

He flipped on a flashlight and placed it on the tent floor, beam directed at the ceiling. By the dim, eery light, he stretched his sleeping bag on the ground and unzipped it, then looked at her expectantly. Reluctantly she surrendered her bag. Arms wrapped around herself, she watched him connect the two separate sleeping bags into one, trying not to think of the inherent symbolism. She was racked by another round of shivers and wondered if the temperature alone accounted for her tremors.

He looked up at her from his position beside the double-size bedroll. "This will work best if we take off some clothes."

Josie's jaw dropped. "B-beg your pardon?"

"Take off your shoes and your jacket. We'll warm up faster if we can feel each other's body heat."

She was beginning to think she could feel his body heat clear across the tent. "I h-hope you know wh-what y-you're doing," she said. She knelt and untied her sneakers with blue fingers, then peeled off her lightweight wool jacket. "Taking off anything wh-when I f-feel this c-c-cold seems downright unnatural."

He gave a grin and sat on the edge of the bedroll, flipped back the top of the sleeping bag and motioned for her to crawl in. Josie awkwardly slid between the covers and lay stiffly on the cold fabric, watching him pull off his cowboy boots. He stripped off his jacket, and her mouth went dry at the sight of his biceps bulging through his flannel shirt.

It was all too unnerving to watch. Swallowing hard, she pressed her eyes closed. Moments later she jerked them open when she felt him leaning over her, arranging something on top of her under the covers. "What are you doing?"

"Placing your jacket over your feet." He fitted himself beside her, then reached down and pulled the zipper, sealing them up together.

Oh, mercy! Her heart pounded as he snuggled against her, smelling like cold air and clean skin, feeling large-boned and hard-muscled and deliciously warm.

He slid one arm under her neck, wrapped the other around her waist and gathered her against his chest. Her fingers landed on crisp hair and naked skin. "Your shirt's open," she gasped.

"I thought it might help you get warmer."

It was definitely doing that, she thought wildly. She had to admit that his chest *was* deliciously toasty—and so were his arms wrapped around her, his legs next to hers, his soft breath on her face. Every inch of him, in fact, seemed wonderfully, wickedly warm.

"You can put your hands inside my shirt to help thaw your fingers," he said.

"I hope you're not expecting me to return the favor," she said dryly.

She could feel the chuckle vibrate in his throat. His hand moved up her back. "No, I'm not expecting it. But a man can dream, can't he?"

Oh, dear. Her pulse roared in her ears as he cradled her against him. She snuggled in, savoring the heat of his body.

"Why don't you put your feet between my legs?" he suggested.

"Right," she replied dryly. "And you can put your elbow in my ear. If you prefer, maybe you could put your knee in my nose."

His white teeth flashed in the indirect glow of the flashlight, his chest rumbling with laughter. She didn't know how he could possibly draw her any closer than she already was, but he somehow managed. "I'm glad your sense of humor isn't as frozen as your toes, Josephine."

Something about hearing her full name on his lips made her stomach quiver. "Well, if we can't laugh about this situation, what else can we do?"

"Do you really want me to answer that?"

The low, sexy sound of his voice by her ear sent a shiver chasing through her. Mistaking her reaction as cold, his arms moved around her. "Are you starting to get warmer?"

"Yes." He was so deliciously, wondrously warm that she was starting to relax in spite of herself. "How about you?"

"Oh, I'm getting warm, all right," he growled. Too warm, in fact. Torturously warm.

Torture—that's what this was, all right, Luke thought grimly. No form of punishment could be more excruciating than lying with this woman in such an intimate fashion, while being restrained from acting on the impulses raging through every fiber of his being. Holding her, inhaling her scent, feeling her hair on his face was sheer, unadulterated torture.

He could feel her heart beating through her sweater, and it set his to racing. He was on fire. In pain. In agony.

And she was...

Asleep. Luke listened to her soft, regular breathing and

tentatively lifted her hand from his chest. It was limp and heavy and lifeless.

She was asleep, all right. Out cold. Completely zonked.

Heck, it was no wonder. She'd been up since dawn helping Consuela in the kitchen, she'd spent the whole day outside, and she probably hadn't slept a lick before she'd ventured outside the tent. She must have been flat-out exhausted.

Still, it rattled his masculine pride that she was able to so thoroughly relax under the circumstances. Did she find him so completely unexciting?

He pulled away just enough to angle a glance down at her, and his breath caught in his throat. The sight of her long, sweeping lashes, her sleep-softened lips, the delicate curve of her chin made his heart turn over.

Without thinking why, he planted a kiss on her silky hair and gathered her close against him. A strong, unexplained tenderness welled up inside of him as he chastely held her in the dark—a tenderness that in its own way was every bit as powerful as the other emotions surging through him.

He buried his nose against her neck and inhaled her soft, flowery scent. His body hard with blazing desire, his heart soft as a toasted marshmallow, he lay wide awake till dawn.

Chapter Eight

Josie slid the sliced fruit off the cutting board and into the serving bowl, then glanced across the lodge kitchen to the table where Consuela sat with her leg propped on a chair, supervising the two kitchen helpers at the stove. "Can I get you anything, Consuela? Another cup of coffee, maybe?"

"*Gracias,* no. I'm fine." The housekeeper's face creased into a smile. "I'm just sorry the weather turned bad, and the rest of your trip was canceled."

"I was so worried about your ankle, I would have wanted to come back anyway. What a relief it's just sprained!"

"*Si,*" Consuela agreed. "But you weren't the only one who was worried. When I woke up this morning and saw how cold it had become, I was inside myself."

Josie smiled. "I think you mean 'beside yourself.'"

The woman nodded. "*Si.* Manuel, he dashed out of the house in a panic to go get you. How did you and Luke manage not to freeze?"

"The, uh, sleeping bags are pretty well insulated," Josie said evasively. She picked up another apple and began assaulting it with a knife. Even if Consuela didn't guess the truth from the blush scorching her cheeks, Manuel was sure to tell her he'd discovered the two of them together in the tent this morning.

Just the thought of it made the temperature of Josie's face escalate a few more degrees. She'd awakened in Luke's arms this morning to the sound of the Jeep outside the tent. Luke had immediately jumped out of the sleeping bag and into his boots, then headed outside. Still, Manuel had to know they'd spent the night in the tent together. And when he'd helped pack up the tent, he'd seen one large, double sleeping bag and had no doubt drawn his own conclusions.

Not that there was anything to conclude. Nothing had happened. In large part because she'd no sooner found herself in Luke's arms than she'd fallen sound asleep.

Well, it was a darn good thing she had, Josie thought, peeling an orange to add to the fruit salad. It was probably her subconscious's way of protecting her. After their conversation last night, her feelings for Luke had shifted to a new, heightened level—a level that made keeping an emotional distance from him harder than ever.

The thought had even crossed her mind that he was the kind of man she could fall in love with. She'd rapidly banished the thought, of course. She wasn't in the market for love. She needed to get her career jump-started and her self-confidence solidified. She needed to get her life in order before she even thought about sharing it with someone else.

Yes, it was a good thing she'd fallen asleep when she had. Because besides the fact that he was dangerous emotionally, he was definitely a physical temptation. Just thinking about his hard, powerful body, his dark, piercing eyes, his delicious, seductive lips was enough to make her joints turn to jelly. Spending the night in his arms had felt far, far too good—even better than she'd imagined, and she'd done quite a bit of imagining along those lines.

Josie gave a dreamy sigh, then realized with embarrassment that Consuela was watching her curiously, a faint smile etched on her mouth. Josie abruptly pulled her thoughts back to the present and busily finished slicing the orange. It was a good thing the two kitchen helpers were working beside her, she thought, or else Consuela would be grilling her like a hamburger.

The two workers headed to the dining room to set up the breakfast buffet just as Luke burst through the kitchen door, pulling his cowboy hat from his head. Josie's heart pounded as his gaze slammed into hers.

Luke felt like he'd just been hit in the stomach. The air whooshed out of his lungs and his belly tightened as his eyes met hers. It had been less than an hour since he'd dropped her at her cabin, yet he couldn't seem to stop looking at her, as if he hadn't seen her in years.

Thank goodness today was her last full day at the ranch. Last night had nearly done him in. She was getting under his skin in a way he had no intention of ever letting a woman do again.

Well, he wouldn't have to worry about that after tomorrow, he told himself. Checkout time was twelve noon. By 12:01 she'd be out of his life for good, and things could finally get back to normal.

The thought left him feeling like a hollowed-out log. The very fact that it did was proof of just how badly he needed to get away from this woman, he told himself.

He gave her a curt nod, then forced his eyes to Consuela. He planted a kiss on the housekeeper's cheek. "I was sure glad to hear you weren't seriously injured, Consuela. But why aren't you home? Manuel said you're supposed to stay off that foot.''

The housekeeper's eyebrows rode high on her forehead as she craned her neck to look up at him. "And who would have seen to breakfast for your guests if I'd stayed home?''

"I would have handled it.''

Consuela rolled her eyes in a way that spoke volumes about her opinion of Luke's cooking abilities. From the corner of the room, he heard Josie laugh.

The sound rankled his already wounded male pride. Not that he gave a rat's tail what Josie thought, he thought obstinately. Not in the least. He just wanted to set the record straight, that was all. "I admit I'm no great shakes in the kitchen, but no one would have starved. I could have rustled up some scrambled eggs and toast.''

"And what would you have done for lunch?''

She had him there. "I guess I'd have gotten one of the boys to barbecue something.'' He shifted a booted foot and jammed a hand in his jeans. "But that's beside the point, Consuela. The point is you need to take it easy.''

"It would be a lot easier to do that if we had a manager for the lodge.''

Luke raked a hand through his hair, his chest tight with frustration. "You know I'm doing my best to find one.''

"Well, I've got the perfect person. Why don't you hire Josie?''

Luke's gaze flew to Josie's face. Her mouth was open, her eyes round and wide. She looked as stunned as he felt.

"I...I don't have the experience to be a general manager,'' Josie sputtered.

"Experience—bah!'' Consuela dismissed the concept with a wave of her hand. "We've had three managers through here who had experience, and what did they do for us?'' Consuela leaned forward and turned her black eyes on Luke. "Josie's got a college degree in hotel and restaurant management, and she went through a fancy training program at that big Chicago hotel. She knows everything she needs to know. Just because she's never held a big title before doesn't mean she isn't qualified. Why, she's already got the staff coming to work and doing their jobs ten times better than before. It's miraculous. Besides, she already knows the lodge."

Luke looked again at Josie. Her face was scarlet, but her eyes were bright and hopeful.

For just a second he allowed himself to feel the same way. Was there a chance it might actually work? Was it possible she'd want to stay on the ranch for keeps?

The next second he was annoyed at his reaction. He was getting soft, he chided himself—soft in the head as well as the heart.

She'd stay just long enough for him to get even more attached to her than he already was, then she'd get bored and leave. The reason she'd been so taken with summer camp as a child was because she'd had limited exposure to it. Her attraction to the ranch would be the same. Once the newness wore off, she'd be anxious to make tracks back to the city.

Josie turned to Consuela. "I appreciate your vote of confidence, but I'm sure Luke wants someone with more references."

"References, schmeferences." Consuela shook her head. "They mean nothing. Luke needs someone who can run the lodge, starting right away. Luke needs *you*. And since you need a job, well, it's a perfect match." She nodded as if the matter were settled, then reached for her crutches. "Now, if you two will excuse me, I must make sure the buffet is all set."

"I'll check it for you," Josie said quickly. "You don't need to get up."

Consuela turned to Luke, her eyebrows curved in an I-told-you-so arch as Josie scurried from the room. "See?"

"Oh, I see, all right," he muttered. "I see that I've been set up."

"I don't know what you mean."

The old minx knew exactly what he meant, but Luke had been around her enough years to know it was pointless to argue. Heaving a sigh, he lowered himself into a chair across the table from her.

"Hiring Josie is the perfect solution," Consuela said.

Luke scowled. "There's nothing perfect about it."

"Give me one good reason it wouldn't work."

"She's a city girl. She doesn't know the first thing about ranching."

"She doesn't need to know about a ranch. She needs to know about a lodge. About that, she knows plenty."

Luke's frown deepened as he raked a hand through his hair. "She knows a lot of management theory. I don't know how good she'd be at handling the actual day-to-day operation."

"She'll be *magnifico*," Consuela said confidently.

"She'll leave as soon as she lands a better job."

"So?" Consuela turned both hands up. "At least we'd have her in the meantime. We need someone right now, while my ankle heals."

Luke gazed at the thick elastic bandages wrapped around Consuela's ankle and ran his hand across his chin. She was right, of course. There was no logical reason not to hire Josie, at least on a temporary basis. And there was no logical reason for the gut-clenching anxiety that gripped his stomach at the very idea, either.

No reason at all, unless he counted the fact that less than

two hours ago he was holding her in his arms as she slept, his body aching, his heart rampaging with wild, incoherent emotions that had left him dazed and confused. Hell, he couldn't even walk into the same room with her without feeling like he'd taken a fist in the gut.

"Besides," Consuela continued, "you have no one now. If she leaves, you'll be in no worse shape than you already are."

He had a sinking feeling he was already in worse shape than he'd been when she'd arrived. The housekeeper might not know it, but she'd just voiced his deepest fear about Josie staying: what would it be like when she left?

But he couldn't explain that to Consuela. Not unless he wanted her to jump to a lot of unwelcome conclusions.

"The lodge is large. It'll be hard for me to check all the rooms on my crutches."

Ah, hell, Luke thought with a pang of guilt, Consuela needed help, and Josie could provide it. Just because he was irrationally, insanely attracted to the woman was no reason to deny the housekeeper the assistance she needed.

But if Josie stayed, there would have to be some ground rules, he told himself firmly. Their relationship would have to remain strictly professional: no socializing, no trail rides, no cookouts, no moonlight encounters of any kind. And definitely, most definitely, no overnight camp outs.

"If you're going to ask her to stay, you better go do it," Consuela advised. "Otherwise she'll think you're repugnant."

"Repugnant?" He stared at her, puzzled, wondering what the heck she was trying to say and if the malapropism was deliberate. It was a question he'd often asked himself over the years. "You must mean reluctant."

And boy, was he ever. But the way he saw it, he had no choice. Injured ankle or not, Consuela would work herself to death if he didn't round up some help, and round it up fast.

He heaved a heavyhearted sigh, placed his hands flat on the table and hauled his long frame to his feet. "All right, Consuela. To help you out, I'll offer her the job on a trial basis. But if it doesn't work out for any reason, she'll be sent packing, and I don't want to hear a word about it."

"Oh ¡bueno! Wonderful!" Consuela clapped her hands together, her round face beaming like a full moon.

Luke slowly headed toward the dining room, as enthusiastic as a dog headed to a flea bath. He sensed movement behind him, and at the kitchen door he paused and looked back.

Consuela was on her feet, moving away from the table. He wasn't sure, but he thought he saw her take a step on her injured foot. She stopped, gave an odd, sheepish grin and leaned heavily on her crutches.

For a woman with an injured ankle, she was getting around awfully fast. Luke's brow furrowed, his doubts from the night before crowding his mind. He stared at her, his hand on the door. "How long did the doctor say you're supposed to stay off that ankle, Consuela?"

"Until it stops hurting."

"And how long might that be?"

Consuela shrugged. "Maybe a few days. Maybe a few weeks."

Maybe until Josie was safely ensconced in her new role. Luke frowned. If he said something along those lines and he turned out to be wrong, he'd feel like a heel. If he said nothing and turned out to be right, he'd feel like a chump. Consuela was no doubt counting on the fact he'd rather be a chump than a heel.

She knew him too well. Hellfire and damnation, he thought darkly, blowing a forceful blast of air through his teeth. With a heavy heart and strong suspicions he was being conned, he stalked off to find Josie.

"This was the last thing in your car," Luke said, placing a small sewing machine on the floor next to a stack of cardboard boxes and suitcases. "Anything else I can do to help you get settled?"

The offer sounded halfhearted at best, and the eager-to-flee expression on his face spoke far louder than his words. He'd sounded equally reluctant when he'd offered her the job, Josie thought. Well, he'd be singing a different tune in a few weeks. She couldn't wait to get to work and show him he hadn't made a mistake in hiring her.

She looked around her new home. Attached to the rear of the lodge, the manager's apartment was small but cozy, furnished in the same rugged style as the rest of the lodge. The quarters came with its own tiny kitchen and a wood-burning fireplace. With the addition of some curtains and a few throw pillows, the place could be charming.

Josie smiled. "I can take it from here. Thanks for helping unload my car."

Luke shook his head as he moved toward the door. "I didn't know a car that size could hold so much stuff."

"I wanted to make the move in one trip so I wouldn't have to run the family gauntlet again."

Luke paused, his hand on the doorknob. "They gave you a hard time?"

Josie shrugged. "About what I expected. I had to listen to all the reasons why this was a terrible idea. Mom begged me to stay in Tulsa. My father tried to persuade me to go to law school so I could take my rightful place in his firm. My sisters rolled their eyes and were full of dire predictions, but in the end, they all hugged me and wished me well. I think they all expect to see me back when my three-month trial period is over.''

Luke's brow furrowed. ''Well, we did agree that the job is only temporary. At the end of three months we'll both reevaluate the situation.''

Josie grinned. ''At the end of three months I hope to have landed a permanent job at another resort or hotel. It's always easier to find a job when you've already got one.'' She widened her smile. ''On the other hand, who knows? At the end of three months, you might be begging me to stay.''

That was exactly what he was afraid of. She might not think so now, but three months was probably the outside limit of how long she'd want to stay. Making the job temporary at least gave him the illusion of being in control.

So did setting definite boundaries. He gave a wan smile. ''There's something else we need to get straight. I don't believe in mixing business with pleasure. From here on out, our relationship will be strictly professional.''

''Good.''

Good? What kind of remark was that? When he heard her give a sigh of relief, it sounded like his ego deflating.

''Believe me, I have no interest in jeopardizing the first job I've managed to land in the hospitality industry after half a year of job hunting,'' she said. ''I want to focus on work and earn a good job reference so I can get my career back on track.''

His jaw twitched. He gave a quick nod. ''Glad we understand each other.''

''Me, too. Good thing we had this little talk.''

''Yeah. Good thing.''

Yeah, right. If it was so all-fired, cotton-pickin' good, he thought as he closed the door behind him, why did he feel so all-fired, cotton-pickin' bad?

* * *

Josie pulled the last page out of the computer printer, tucked it in a file folder and headed out of the lodge office to find someone who could tell her Luke's whereabouts. She knew better than to expect to find him at the lodge; he'd made himself scarcer than hens' teeth during the week since she'd been on the job.

They'd agreed to keep their relationship strictly professional, but Luke was taking this to extremes. Not socializing was one thing; avoiding her entirely was quite another. He was her boss, and she couldn't do her job without at least occasionally consulting him on business matters.

She found Consuela in the main hall, a crutch slung under one arm, dusting the mantel of the gigantic fireplace under the star-patterned quilt. Josie gazed up at it, her thoughts flying to Luke and their conversation during the camp out. Despite her resolve, the memory churned up a host of very unbusinesslike feelings.

She deliberately thrust them aside. "Consuela, do you have any idea where I can find Luke this morning? I have a stack of things I need to go over with him."

The housekeeper nodded. "He said he had some paperwork to do. That means he's at his office."

"At his house?"

"*Sí.*"

The idea of visiting Luke at his home made Josie's stomach clench. "Maybe I should wait for him to come here."

Consuela gave a lopsided grin. "The way he's been avoiding this place, you could still be waiting come next July."

So she wasn't the only one who'd noticed Luke's sparse appearances at the lodge, Josie thought grimly.

"Everyone goes to the house to discuss business with Luke," Consuela said. "It was the ranch headquarters long before this lodge was built. Manuel goes there to see him about ranch business all the time. So did the other lodge managers before you.''

She had questions that needed answers, projects that needed his approval, Josie firmly told herself. She couldn't allow her personal feelings to prevent her from getting her work accomplished. ''All right. Can you tell me how to get there?''

The house was a mile from the lodge, but it was such a beautiful day that Josie decided to walk. Following Consuela's directions, she set out along a narrow gravel road through the woods.

The fall foliage was rapidly dropping from the trees, completely changing the way the scenery had looked when she'd first arrived at the ranch. So many things had changed since then, she mused. Two weeks ago she had no faith in her own judgment, she'd given up on her career and she was about to marry a man she didn't even know she didn't love. But another event loomed in her mind as an even bigger change.

Two weeks ago, she hadn't met Luke O'Dell.

The thought rattled her like the wind on the dry leaves. Blowing out a harsh breath, she increased her pace. Luke had stayed on her mind as persistently as a flea on a dog ever since she'd first met him, but her thoughts about him had taken on a new dimension ever since the camp out. Since then, she'd felt something uncomfortably close to tenderness.

It was all perfectly understandable, she rationalized. Hearing him talk about his mother's death had given her an insight into him that would have touched anyone's heart. She wasn't a psychologist, but it didn't take one to realize he was struggling with some deep-seated feelings of abandonment. His mother had died, his father had emotionally withdrawn from him, his wife had left him. It was no wonder he tried to keep his emotional distance from people, Josie thought. He was probably afraid to open his heart to anyone.

Which was exactly why it touched her so that he'd opened up and talked to her.

She was reading too much into it, she told herself. Under similar circumstances, with moonlight, solitude and a cozy campfire, he probably would have confided in anyone.

Besides, it didn't matter, anyway. He was her employer now, and there was no room in a business relationship for the kind of thoughts and feelings she'd been having about him. She had her work cut out just trying to convince him she could manage the lodge.

He sure hadn't seemed any too eager to hire her. When he'd offered her the job, he'd prefaced it with all the reasons she probably wouldn't want to take it. When she'd accepted it, anyway, he'd looked less than elated.

She knew he'd only hired her to placate Consuela, but she'd jumped at the offer. Working at the ranch would give her the chance to earn a job reference and allow her to get on with her career. It would help her establish her independence and give her a place to stay.

And it would allow her to continue to have some contact with Luke, a tiny voice deep inside reminded her.

Josie shook her head, trying to dislodge the troublesome thought. Accepting the job had been a good, solid decision based on good, solid logic, and she wasn't going to second-guess her judgment in making it, she thought firmly. Her parents had done more than enough of that for her when she'd gone to Tulsa to pick up her belongings. As she'd explained to them, the job was an ideal opportunity, and she intended to make the most of it.

Filled with fresh resolve, she rounded a curve in the trail and spotted an imposing two-story structure at the end of a long, tree-lined drive. Made of whitewashed brick, the old plantation-style house was wrapped with upper and lower covered galleries, each lined with six pairs of French doors flanked by long, black shutters.

A swarm of butterflies fluttered in Josie's stomach as she mounted the wide steps of the porch and raised her hand to the large brass door knocker. The door stood slightly ajar and swung open as she knocked on it.

"Come in," Luke bellowed from deep inside the structure.

Josie hesitantly stepped into the foyer, taking in the polished hardwood floor, the chandelier over the curved staircase, the classic furnishings. Josie didn't know exactly what she'd expected the house to look like—maybe a smaller version of the lodge—but this was far more elegant than anything she'd imagined.

Clutching the folder she'd brought with her, she headed toward the center of the house, peering into open doorways until she found him seated behind a massive desk in a large, book-lined room, his head bent over a stack of papers.

"Manuel, have you seen the invoice for the—" Luke looked up and blinked in surprise. "Josie."

He pushed himself out of his chair, his heart unaccountably picking up speed as he stared at her. He had a hard time recalling exactly why he'd gone to such lengths to avoid her all week. In that tailored red dress, she looked hotter than Consuela's five-alarm chili.

Suddenly remembering his manners, he rounded the desk and pulled out a chair for her. "What can I do for you?"

"I need to discuss a few business matters with you," she said, adjusting her skirt as she sat in the chair.

He watched her cross her knees, following the motion like a man in a trance. Jumpin' Jehoshaphat, she had great legs. He'd never seen them before, he thought distractedly.

But then he'd never seen her in a dress before, either—not counting her mud-plastered wedding gown.

The thought reminded him of all the reasons he had no business sitting here ogling her. She was already hounding his thoughts like a hunting dog, making it hard for him to think straight or get a decent night's sleep; the last thing he needed to do was gather more material for his imagination.

"You have a lovely home," she remarked.

"Would you like to see it?" he asked impulsively, anxious to do something, anything to quell the maelstrom of emotions churning inside of him.

"I'd love to." Her smile blinded him like staring into the sun.

He escorted her through the house, telling her about the history of the furnishings, listening to her murmurs of admiration with more pleasure than he should prudently feel, getting more and more caught up in the role of tour guide. The next thing he knew, they were standing in the hallway outside the last upstairs bedroom.

Too late, he tried to steer her away.

"Is this your room?" She brushed past him and peered inside.

Josie gazed around in surprise. It was absolutely immaculate. No piles of dirty clothes, no littered dresser tops, no beer bottles or pizza boxes or other signs of bachelorhood disarray. In fact, the most telling detail about the room was its very lack of personal effects or disorder of any kind. The large oak dresser, the matching chest of drawers and the corner desk were all devoid of any items at all.

The other bedrooms in the house were all tastefully decorated with colorful bedspreads and pillows and pictures, she mused. How odd that Luke's was so spartan.

Beyond spartan—barren. Barren, lonely and somehow

forlorn. Most depressing of all was the large, heavy bed, draped in a drab, faded army blanket.

"Where's your bedspread?" Josie asked.

Luke shrugged. "I haven't used one in years."

"Why not?"

He shifted his stance and shoved a hand in his jeans. "Never found one I liked, I guess. Consuela brought home a different one every week for a while there, but none of them seemed to look right."

Josie's throat suddenly constricted with emotion. *The quilt.* He hadn't used a cover on his bed since the quilt wore out.

No wonder none of the bedspreads had looked right—that quilt had been tailor-made for him, personalized with his name and a special message. None of the replacements would have felt right, either, she thought. The quilt had been made with love. Love had been tucked into the stuffing, stitched in every seam, woven into the very fabric. A store-bought model would seem like a cold, pathetic substitute.

Luke would rather do without than have a poor imitation, she realized, her heart warming and expanding. She wondered if he had any idea how telling that was about his character.

She looked around the colorless room, and everything about it seemed suddenly telling, too. Nothing was out in the open. Everything was hidden in a drawer or tucked in the closet or pushed beneath the bed.

The man who slept there was just like the room, she suddenly realized. He tried to keep his feelings out of sight, too. He didn't want anyone to see inside him, to know him, to be able to touch him.

She fought a strong, absurd urge to open his closet doors, to empty his dresser drawers on the floor, to do something to shatter his sense of control and order. But that would only make him angry, she thought sadly; it wouldn't touch his deeper feelings, wouldn't free him from the thing that kept him emotionally locked up and shut down: a deep-rooted fear of abandonment.

She looked around the bleak, colorless room, and her heart ached to help him.

A quilt. The idea struck with sudden clarity. She'd make him another quilt. She would pattern it after the one in the lodge, and she'd surprise him with it at Christmas.

The idea made her pulse quicken, and her thoughts started racing as she followed him back downstairs to his study and reseated herself in the chair across from his desk. She'd brought her sewing machine from Tulsa, intending to make some curtains and throw pillows for her small apartment. She could buy some fabric and quilt batting in Tahlequah, and...

"What did you want to see me about?" Luke asked, seating himself behind his desk.

With an effort Josie forced her thoughts back to the business at hand. "Your marketing plans."

"I don't have any marketing plans."

"That's exactly why we need to discuss them." Josie smiled, but received only a wary look in return. She opened her folder. "I've reviewed the bookings for the next few months, as well as the monthly occupancy reports for the past two years." She handed him two impressive looking charts.

Luke stared at them. "I've never seen these before. Where'd you get them?"

"I made them." He shot her a surprised look. "On the computer," she added.

Luke studied them, as impressed with Josie's computer skills as he was with her initiative. He had a PC here in his office that he used to handle the ranch's bookkeeping and inventory control, but it was a different system than the one his father had installed at the lodge. The fanciest thing he knew how to do on his computer was line up a ledger column.

Josie leaned across the desk and pointed to a dip on the charts. The scent of her perfume made it hard to follow what she was saying, and it took all of his willpower to force his eyes away from the neckline of her dress and onto the paper in his hand.

"As you can see, the lodge has a pattern of low occupancy during the winter months," she said.

He felt a keen sense of disappointment when she pulled back and reseated herself in her chair. "To counter that, I propose that we market the ranch as a site for small corporate meetings. We could easily offer team building programs."

"Team what?"

"Outings that help management teams bond with each other. I contacted a management training company in Tulsa that conducts these programs, and one of their executives visited the ranch yesterday. He thinks the Lazy O is a perfect site, and he agreed to participate in some joint advertising programs with us."

"But we don't do any advertising."

Josie smiled and pulled out another chart. "Which brings me to my next topic."

She proceeded to methodically lay out all the reasons they needed to advertise, then launched into a carefully thought-out marketing plan. By the time she finished, his head was swimming with time lines, budgets and projected returns on investment.

It all sounded good—too good, he thought grimly. He knew it was irrational, but the idea of the lodge full to bursting with guests all-year-round filled him with cold dread instead of delight. And the thought of Josie being this smart and effective at her job made his stomach churn. He didn't want to admire her, didn't want to rely on her, didn't want to need her in any way.

He knit his brow into a frown. "I can't make a decision on all this today," he said curtly. "I'll need time to think it over."

"We don't have much time if we want to meet the deadlines for some of the prime publications. I'll need a decision by the end of the week."

Luke didn't like being pushed, didn't like being pressured, didn't like being manipulated. As a matter of fact, he didn't like anything about this entire situation. "You'll get a decision when I'm good and ready to arrive at one." He rose from his chair in a clear signal their meeting was over. "Is there anything else you need from me today? Because if you're finished, I've got a stack of work I need to see to."

He directed his attention back to the pile of papers in front of him, not bothering to escort her to the door as she left. She'd found her own way in, by golly, and she could find her own way out. He hadn't asked her to come here, and he had better things to do than play nursemaid to her.

Scowling, he picked up the stack of invoices he'd been perusing when she'd interrupted. But he couldn't get her off his mind. For the rest of the morning, he wondered why that hurt look in her eyes had made his chest tighten like a cinched saddle and why he felt lower than the bottom of Black Star's hooves.

Chapter Nine

Josie opened the door of her apartment. "Luke!" she said, surprised.

She was framed in light as she stood in the doorway, and Luke thought she looked as dazzling as an angel atop a Christmas tree. She wasn't wearing anything special, just a loose gray sweat suit, but she had the same effect on Luke's pulse rate now as she'd had in that red dress she'd worn to his house last week.

Had it only been a week? It felt like a lot longer.

He drank in the sight of her like a man dying of thirst, then abruptly realized he was staring. He shifted his hat to his other hand. "I know it's late. I hope I'm not disturbing you."

"No...not at all. I was just sewing and watching TV." She opened the door wider. "Come on in."

Luke stepped inside and gazed around in surprise. The small apartment looked completely different, but he couldn't figure out why. The furniture was all the same. "What did you do to this place?"

She grinned. "Made some curtains and throw pillows, hung some pictures, brought in some plants."

She'd really settled in, he thought, as if she were going to stay. The thought filled him with an odd hope, and the reaction alarmed him.

She would only be here long enough to land another job, he warned himself. If he had any sense, he'd be wishing she'd get the heck out of here as soon as possible and leave him in peace.

That was what he'd originally wanted—wasn't it? He was no longer sure of anything he'd ever thought or felt where she was concerned. He frowned, wondering what the heck was happening to him.

He felt her eyes on him and forced a smile. "The place looks nice."

"Thanks."

A sewing machine on the dining table caught his eye. "Making more curtains?"

"No. It's a...a...crafts project." She darted over, gathered up the multicolored scraps of fabric stacked beside the machine and stuffed them into a plastic bag. "Excuse the mess. I wasn't expecting company."

She seemed oddly flustered. It was probably rude of him to just drop in like this, but he'd needed to talk to her, and he hadn't wanted to say what he had to say over the phone. Luke hooked a thumb in his front pocket and decided to get down to the purpose of his visit. "I got the message you left on my answering machine that you needed to see me. I figure it's about the advertising." Luke swallowed hard. He was trying to eat some crow, and it wasn't going down very easily. "I'm, uh, sorry it's taken me a while to get back to you, but I've been really busy."

Right, O'Dell, he mentally derided himself. Busy trying not to think about her. Busy trying to forgive himself for being a jerk to her at the house. Busy fighting off the urge to come see her. "Anyway, I dropped by to tell you I've thought it over and you can go ahead with your plans."

"You like them?"

"Well, *like* might be too strong a word," he hedged. "I'm not too keen on anything that has to do with the lodge. Let's just say you made a valid case for it."

"You won't be sorry."

He'd ended up sorry about nearly everything he'd said or done ever since she'd arrived at the ranch, he thought sardonically. Why should this be any different?

"Let's just give it a try and see how it goes."

Josie smiled and sat down on the sofa, patting a place beside her. "Thanks for the vote of confidence. But that isn't why I called."

He lowered himself beside her. "It isn't?"

"No. I found something on the computer that you need to see." Her voice held a quiet, somber note he'd never heard before, and the serious expression on her face alarmed him.

She picked up a thick stack of papers from the coffee table and held them out to him. "Luke, your father kept a journal. I discovered it this morning when I was going through the computer files."

Luke's heart thudded and stopped, then resumed beating at an erratic pace. "A journal? You mean like a diary?"

Josie nodded.

Luke stared at the papers as if they might bite. His arm felt heavy and stiff and seemed to move in slow motion as he reached out to take them from her.

He saw the sympathy in her eyes and wondered why it was there. Because she knew he was nervous about reading his father's words, or because she already knew what he'd written?

"Have you read it?" he asked abruptly.

Josie hesitated, then nodded, her eyes apologetic. "I know I shouldn't have. I started reading it before I knew what it was, and then, well... I just couldn't stop. I'm sorry. It was an invasion of privacy, and—"

"I don't care about that." The content of the damned thing was what had his stomach in knots. What if it confirmed what he'd always feared—that his dad blamed him for the accident?

The room suddenly seemed too warm, the open collar of his shirt too tight. He gazed down at the papers, and the words seemed to swim on the page like letters in a bowl of alphabet soup. He couldn't bear to read it. He swallowed again, his Adam's apple jerking in his throat. "So what does it say?"

He clenched his jaw and braced himself, wondering wildly if he should tell her to never mind, that he really didn't want to know. Maybe he should just take the blasted thing out and burn it, or bury it until he felt ready to deal with it. A hundred years or so should do the trick.

"Maybe you should take it home and read it when you're alone," she suggested gently.

He felt her hand on his, and raised his eyes from the papers to her face. Her gaze was warm, her eyes soft and comforting. Whatever the news, he could trust her to break it gently.

He grasped her hand and spoke in a voice like rough gravel. "I'd rather hear it from you."

Her eyes took on added depth, like a sapphire turned in the light. She returned the pressure of his hand. "Your father loved you, Luke. He built the lodge because he didn't want you to end up like him."

"What?" The word came out cracked and low.

"He was afraid you were going to deal with your divorce

from Cheryl like he dealt with your mother's death—by isolating yourself and shutting everyone out." Josie laid her other hand on top of his, sandwiching his between. "He knew he was in bad health, Luke. He built the lodge so you'd be forced to deal with people."

"What do you mean?"

"He knew you'd be surrounded by people if you had to run a lodge," she repeated. "He was worried that you'd turn into too much of a loner if you only worked the ranch."

Luke stared in silence, trying to take it in. "That old son of a gun," he finally murmured. His mind seized on another thing she'd just said. "He knew he was going to die?"

"He knew his heart was bad."

Luke leaned back on the pillows, trying to absorb it all.

"He blamed himself for your mother's death, Luke," Josie continued softly. "He thought he should have gone with you that day, that he should have been driving the car. His feelings of guilt and grief paralyzed him. The distance between the two of you just kept getting wider and wider, and by the time he pulled himself together enough to realize what was happening, the distance was so great, he didn't know how to close it." Josie's hand tightened on his. "But he loved you, Luke. He built the lodge because he loved you."

His father had loved him. He hadn't blamed him for his mother's death.

Luke sat perfectly still and stared at Josie, hearing her words, but not yet emotionally comprehending them. It didn't seem real. The only thing he was sure was real were her light blue eyes, filled with warmth and concern and compassion.

He finally lowered his gaze to the pages she'd printed from the computer and started reading. Josie sat close beside him, reading along with him, occasionally pointing out something she'd mentioned.

Thirty minutes later he set down the last page. "Well, I'll be damned," he muttered.

He hadn't been rejected, he hadn't been blamed. He'd only been a victim of his father's grief and depression. His chest was a tight jumble of emotion. Sorrow for his father's pain and loneliness, remorse that he hadn't understood, regret that they'd been unable to connect and comfort each other—and overriding it all, a deep, vast sense of relief and freedom. A millstone he'd unfairly carried for twenty years had been dropped from around his neck.

"Are you okay?" Josie asked softly.

Her eyes were the sweet, welcome blue of the sky after a storm, and his heart fluttered at the sight like a caged bird longing to be set free. He nodded, not yet trusting himself to speak, and wondered how much of the emotion churning in him was sadness, how much was relief and how much was gratitude.

"This is all going to take some getting used to," he finally managed to say. "It puts a lot of things in a new light."

And one of those things was how he felt about her, he realized. He'd wanted her—no, he'd *needed* her—with him when he learned the truth about his father's feelings for him. When she'd held his hand, he'd felt warmed and comforted and strengthened. When she'd looked in his eyes, he'd felt cared about. When she was beside him, he felt less alone than he'd felt in years. She made him feel connected and close, and he ached to get still closer.

No, a voice in his head warned him. Jeez'em Pete and Gladys, she was already as close as his own skin. She'd wedged her way into nooks and crannies of his being that no one else had touched. He'd never intended to let anyone get this close again. People got close, then they left. He never wanted to risk getting hurt that way again.

He glanced at her and felt his heart turn over, his resolve flattening out like one of Consuela's tortillas. He wanted to pull her into his arms, and the warm, inviting light in her eyes told him she wanted the same thing. How much harm could there be in a simple hug?

A lot. He wasn't thinking clearly. His mind was muddled with all this new information. He didn't need to hug her. He needed to leave. He forced himself to his feet and headed for the door. She rose with him.

He lifted the stack of papers. "Thanks for giving this to me."

"You're welcome."

"Well, I owe you."

"I'll try to think of a way to make you pay," she said lightly.

"Be sure and make me pay big."

"How big?" She gave a winsome smile. "Because I've got something in mind."

"Name it."

"All right." Josie drew a deep breath. "How would you like to escort me to the Renaissance Ball in Tulsa in three weeks? My parents are on the board of directors, and it would go a long way toward mending fences in my own backyard."

"Your folks are still unhappy you took this job?"

Josie nodded ruefully. "But I don't think the issue is the job, or even the fact I moved away. I think they're afraid of not being needed." Josie's brows drew together, her face serious. "Your father's journal made me do some thinking about my relationship with my parents. I want to let them know that they'll always be an important part of my life, regardless of where I'm living or what I'm doing. Showing up at an event that's so important to them seems like a good way to do that.''

He gave a slow nod. "You're wise to mend your fences before they fall down. You can't always assume that the people you love know it.''

The words hung between them, suspended in the air, which was suddenly thick with tension. Something in her eyes made the breath catch in his throat.

His gaze slid to her lips, and he silently gauged the distance between them. One step would just about do it. Oh, criminy, it was tempting. Just one step, and she could be in his arms.

No. If he kissed her now, it would have far-ranging consequences. Even if he hadn't just made that remark about love, they'd shared something moving and profound and deeply personal tonight, and a kiss in its wake would be more than a mere kiss.

He gazed down at her, his heart catapulting at the way she gazed back. He struggled to form a clear thought.

He couldn't kiss her, but he *did* owe her a favor.

"If you're sure I won't embarrass you, you've got yourself a date.''

He yanked open the door, then hesitated as another thought struck him. Was she wanting him to go with her in order to make her ex-fiancé jealous? He wouldn't be suckered into that role again.

He turned in the doorway. "Is Robert going to be there?''

"No. He quit his job at Dad's firm and moved to Dallas a week after the wedding was canceled.''

So her ex was completely out of the picture. A broad sense of relief swept Luke's chest. With a short nod he ducked out the door.

Josie watched it close behind him. For one heart-stopping

moment, she'd been certain he was going to kiss her. Almost as certain as she'd been earlier that he'd needed her tonight.

She was still certain of that. She rubbed her hands along her arms, a thrill chasing through her. Independent, stubborn, lone-wolf Luke O'Dell had needed her. He'd clung to her hand, he'd rejected her suggestion he read the journal alone, he'd wanted her to break the news to him.

It was shocking how the simple fact that Luke had needed her filled her soul, how it made her heart seem somehow close to bursting. Just as shocking was how much she'd wanted to be there for him, to hold him, to soothe the turmoil she'd seen in his eyes.

Josie abruptly turned away from the door, still rubbing her arms. She was getting in too deep, she warned herself. Her feelings for Luke were growing more irrational and more unreasonable with every encounter. Asking him to take her to the ball was asking for nothing but trouble.

Still, Josie couldn't keep from smiling as she headed back to the sewing machine and pulled out the scraps of fabric to resume working on the quilt. Because the prospect of trouble suddenly had an enormous amount of appeal, and she found herself looking forward to it with a great deal of anticipation.

"Josie, dear, there's someone I want you to meet." Mrs. Randall's elegant chiffon gown billowed around her as she flitted across the hotel ballroom, a bulky, bug-eyed man in tow. "This is Mr. Atkins, the manager of that large, new hotel downtown. Mr. Atkins, this is the daughter I've been telling you about and her friend, Luke O'Dell. Since all three of you are in the hospitality business, I'm sure you have a lot to talk about." The carefully coiffed, meticulously groomed older woman smiled, batted her eyes and sashayed away.

The beefy man barely acknowledged Luke's presence. Taking the hand Josie extended, he held it an extraordinarily long time, hungrily eyeing her like a morsel of prime rib.

Luke did a slow burn, but Josie didn't even seem to notice the way she was being ogled. She was too busy answering Atkins's question about her experience in the hotel industry.

He couldn't blame the man for staring, Luke brooded. Josie was flat-out gorgeous in that black dress. Her hair was pulled back from her face and fell in graceful curls around her shoulders. Each time she moved, her rhinestone earrings shimmered in the light and her perfume wafted tantalizingly in the air.

She was wearing a different scent tonight—something heady and intoxicating, something more sophisticated than what she usually wore.

But then, everything about her tonight seemed more sophisticated. Luke frowned. Seeing her in this lavish setting, surrounded by her elegantly attired and exquisitely well-mannered family, revived his initial impression of her. She was a city slicker of the first order, born and bred for urban life. It was impossible to imagine her parents or sisters or in-laws with mud on their shoes or straw in their hair. They'd be as out of place in a rural setting as Black Star would be in a tuxedo.

His heart sank as he thought about it. Her family had welcomed him warmly, but they lived in a world so far removed from the Lazy O they might as well be from another planet. Whether she wanted to admit it or not, Josie was a part of that world, and it was just a matter of time before she grew bored and wanted to return to it. He was out of his mind, hoping she'd want to permanently stay on the ranch.

A cold, empty spot ached in his chest, a spot he'd mistakenly begun to let Josie fill.

And he *had* been hoping she'd stay, he silently admitted. Ever since she'd given him his father's journal, he'd begun to think that maybe he'd been wrong about her. Maybe she wasn't just enjoying the novelty of the ranch. Maybe she really did like the life-style—hard work, long hours, remote location and all.

After that evening at her apartment, he'd decided one thing for sure—he couldn't go on avoiding her. It was too awkward, too uncomfortable and too damn difficult. So he'd stopped going out of his way to keep his distance.

He'd no sooner stopped avoiding her than he'd found himself actively seeking her out.

For the past two weeks they'd eaten together every evening in the lodge kitchen—much to the delight of Consuela, who was now fully recovered from her accident. They frequently went on walks and trail rides, and he'd even taken her to Tahlequah for dinner and a movie the last two weekends in a row.

The more time he spent with her, the more time he *wanted* to spend with her. When he wasn't with her, he was thinking about her, and when he wasn't thinking about her, he was dreaming about her. She'd even managed to invade his sleep.

"Sounds like you've got exactly the type of background I'm looking for," Luke heard the man tell her. "We could use someone like you on our staff. Your mother indicated you might be interested in a new position."

Possessiveness surged through Luke with sudden ferocity. "She's working for me at the moment."

Mr. Atkins turned disdainful pale eyes in his direction. "Oh? And where might that be?"

"Luke owns a wonderful guest ranch on the Illinois River," Josie replied.

"How interesting," Mr. Atkins said, making it sound like anything but. "Your mother did mention that you have some kind of temporary job arrangement."

Luke struggled to hold his temper in check. "She's committed to work for me until February."

Why, oh why hadn't he made it for longer? He'd been a fool to insist on that "temporary" clause in their agreement, he berated himself.

I don't want to lose her. The thought hit him like a bullwhip, catching him by surprise, jarring him with the force of its impact.

He searched his mind for a way to rationalize it.

From a purely professional standpoint, there were lots of practical reasons to want her to stay. She had the lodge running like a well-oiled engine, and she'd managed to eliminate most of the things about it that Luke had found most irritating. Occupancy was up, expenses were down, and guest satisfaction was at an all-time high.

From a personal standpoint, the reasons were a lot less practical, but just as compelling. She was kind and smart, she had a great sense of humor and she was the most appealing woman he'd ever known. The more he got to know her, the more beautiful she became.

He couldn't look at her, he couldn't think about her without wanting to pull her into his arms and do a thousand forbidden things. It was hell keeping his hands off her. So far he'd managed, but it was becoming harder and harder not to touch her. If he touched her, he was afraid he'd lose all control.

He was burning to touch her tonight. Her scent filled his

head with all kinds of erotic ideas, and the way she looked in that dress made his temperature skyrocket. She'd wanted to dance earlier and he'd turned her down, not trusting himself to hold her.

Something Atkins was saying yanked Luke's attention back to the present. "Our hotel won't even be open until February," the large man told Josie. "This could work out beautifully for both of us."

The jerk was trying to steal Josie right out from under his nose! Luke's fingers curled into fists. He needed to get her away from him, and he needed to do it fast.

The orchestra struck the opening notes of a slow ballad. "This is one of my favorite songs. Let's dance," Luke urged her.

Josie stared at him in surprise. "But you told me you never dance."

Luke silently cursed himself for the lame excuse he'd given her earlier. "Yeah, well, this song is an exception. Come on."

Atkins shot Luke an annoyed look, his lip curled in displeasure, then turned back to Josie. "Here's my card." He pressed it into her hand. "Call me and we'll finish our discussion."

Luke placed his palm on the small of her back and hustled her away. "You wouldn't really consider working for that old lech, would you?"

"Old lech? He's not much older than you are! Besides, he's only interested in my job skills."

"Your skills weren't what he was staring at."

He was jealous. The thought made Josie's heart skip a beat. He wouldn't be jealous if he didn't care, she thought. A smile tugged at the corner of her mouth as she followed him through the throngs of people to the dance floor.

They'd spent a lot of time together over the past three

weeks, but it was hard for her to gauge his feelings for her. She knew he enjoyed her company, he appreciated her sense of humor and—most importantly—he trusted her judgment. But he hadn't so much as held her hand since the night she'd shared the journal with him.

She'd begun to wonder if the incredible attraction she felt was one-sided. Surely she wasn't imagining the way he looked at her or the electricity in the air between them.

His little display of jealousy had just erased all doubts, she thought with satisfaction as they reached the dance floor. And his sharp intake of breath as she stepped into his arms confirmed it.

She fitted herself against him and closed her eyes, letting sensation after delicious sensation wash over her—his breath tickling her ear, the corded muscle of his shoulder beneath her fingers, his hard chest flattening her breasts. She wasn't sure if the thudding in her chest was his heart or her own. Maybe it was both, beating in rhythm together.

His hand moved across her back to the spot where her dress dipped and plunged, and his fingers caressed her bare flesh. A shiver of pleasure raced through her. She moved her hand to the nape of his neck, longing to feel her fingers on his naked skin, too. Her mouth went dry, her pulse roared in her ear, and a pure, single thought crystalized in her mind.

I love him.

The thought made her freeze and falter, causing him to step on her foot.

"Sorry." He gazed down, his eyes dark with concern. "Are you okay?"

She nodded her head, but she wasn't at all sure. The only thing she was sure of was the truth vibrating in her heart.

She was in love with Luke. The realization left her weak-kneed and dizzy, and she was glad his arms were around her for support.

Exactly when or how had it happened? She didn't know, but it was no wonder. There were so many things about him to love—his sense of responsibility, his integrity, his respect for tradition, even his pain over the rift with his father. All of it proved that beneath Luke's gruff exterior beat a kind, caring heart.

A heart that she loved. The knowledge flowed through her like the strains of the music, singing through her veins, dancing in her blood.

But with it came a question: could Luke put the past behind him, open his heart and dare to love again?

She put her head against his shoulder and moved with him across the dance floor, inhaling the faint scent of his cologne, feeling his breath on her neck and his heart against her own, and the question echoed in her mind like a haunting refrain.

Could Luke love her in return?

The laughing, flirtatious conversation she and Luke had enjoyed on the long drive home had settled into silence by the time he steered the pickup into the entrance of the ranch. A steamy ballad played on the radio, and the night was rife with possibilities.

Josie cast a sidelong glance at Luke's profile and felt a thrill of anticipation rush through her. For what, exactly, she couldn't say. She only knew that after that first dance, the rest of the evening had passed in a hazy pink glow. She and Luke had stayed on the dance floor, swaying together, until the orchestra had packed up for the evening. Then Luke had put his arm around her and murmured, "Let's go home."

An undercurrent in his voice had made her shiver. He

wasn't suggesting they end the evening, but continue it in private. Her lips had trembled as she'd smiled up at him and nodded.

When she'd hugged her parents goodbye, her mother had surprised her by inviting Luke to join the family for Thanksgiving dinner. And when Luke went to get her coat, her oldest sister had pulled her aside and with a frankly appreciative glance at Luke had whispered, "Now we know why you don't want to leave that ranch."

Her family seemed to be giving her their blessings, she thought as she sneaked another glance at him now.

Everything, absolutely everything about the evening had been perfect. And the rest of the night still lay ahead.

Her pulse pounded as he stopped the truck at the side of the lodge in front of her small apartment. Her blood felt fevered, and she hardly noticed the autumn chill as he walked her to the door. But she did notice the dark, smoky look in his eyes. Her heart fluttered and raced as she fumbled in her tiny bag for her key. "Would you like to come in for some coffee?"

"I'd like to come in, Josie, but not for coffee."

The flutters became a tempest, and her hand shook as she unlocked the door and stepped inside. She'd left a small lamp burning on the far side of the living room, and the red gingham lampshade cast a dim, rosy glow across the room.

He closed the door behind him, and the sudden intimacy of the situation made her lose her nerve. In a sudden flurry of activity, she took off her jacket, crossed the room and hung it in the coat closet.

When she turned around, he was close behind her, close enough that she could feel his breath on her face. She gave an unsteady smile and tried for a normal tone. "Thanks for taking me tonight. It meant a lot to my parents that I was there.''

"They're nice people.''

Tension quivered in the air between them, and their eyes carried on a conversation that had nothing to do with the topic under discussion. She swallowed convulsively. "They liked you, too. I've never known my mother to invite someone she'd just met to a holiday dinner.''

"That was kind of her.''

They stood there, their eyes still talking, attraction crackling and smoking in air that suddenly seemed too thick to breath. He placed his hands on her bare arms, and she shivered.

"Are you cold?'' he asked.

She gave a tremulous grin. "The last time you asked that, we ended up in a sleeping bag together.''

The corners of his mouth quirked upward. "Not a bad idea.'' He ran his hands down the length of her arms, then up again. The pleasure of it raised goose bumps on her skin. "But I had something else in mind for tonight.''

The look in his eyes was hot enough to melt her bones. A wave of heat unfurled in her belly, sending another shiver chasing through her.

"Josie.'' Her name drifted out as a hungry, needy growl. His arms slipped around her and he moved nearer, closing the scant distance between them. "Josie…''

His lips touched hers like butterfly wings, barely making contact, fluttering away, then descending for another soft taste. The gentleness of it made her blood roar.

She loved him. The knowledge warmed her, filled her, flowed through her. She opened her eyes and found his face hovering over hers, his eyes dark and hungry. The feel of his lips on hers was suddenly as essential as oxygen. With a moan she wound a hand in his hair and pulled his head down.

He kissed her like a man possessed. His lips set her on fire, reducing her to a molten, liquid core of longing. She moved against him, molding herself to him, feeling his desire, feeling it stoke her own. His hands moved to the sides of her breasts, and she thought she would go up in flames.

Abruptly he pulled back. "Josie, honey..." He drew a deep gulp of air. "Josie—we need to talk."

Talk was not what she needed at the moment. She gazed up, her vision blurred. "About what?"

"About the future."

Oh, mercy—he was going to propose! The thought set her heart gladly, madly pounding against her ribs. "What about it?" she whispered.

"What are your plans for after the first of the year?"

Josie looked away, struggling to play it cool. "I...I haven't really made any plans."

"Well, you must have some idea where you want to go from here."

Directly to bed, by way of the nearest marriage license bureau. Do not pass go. She opened her mouth, then closed it. This was a moment she knew she'd remember all her life, and she was old-fashioned enough to want him to do the asking. She dropped her eyes, suddenly shy. "Well, I...I thought I'd wait and see what opportunities present themselves."

Luke stared at her, feeling like he'd been dowsed by a bucket of cold water. His joints stiffened and his heart seemed to freeze in his chest.

It was just as he'd feared—she was only marking time at the ranch until she landed another job. As soon as she did, she'd be gone. And from the sound of her conversation with that Atkins jerk tonight, it wouldn't be much longer.

His jaw tensed, and a muscle flexed in it. "I see."

"See what?" she asked, her eyes wide and confused.

It was what he'd figured would happen from the very beginning, he told himself, his fingers knotting into tight, white-knuckled fists at his side. Seeing her in her natural element tonight should have confirmed it. So why did he feel like he'd just been sucker punched in the gut?

He stalked stiffly to the door. "It's late. I'd better go." He twisted the knob and strode out.

She called his name as he climbed into the truck, but he pretended not to hear her—just as he pretended not to see her standing in the doorway as he started the engine, jerked the gearshift and drove off in a spray of gravel.

There was no point in dragging things out. There was no possibility of a future between them. Never had been, never could be. He clenched his teeth so hard his jaw hurt. He'd been a fool to ever think otherwise. It had been a sure bet she would leave from the moment she arrived.

Well, thank heavens he'd kept his distance, he told himself. It was a damned good thing he hadn't gotten all emotionally involved with her.

But his hollow, aching heart didn't buy it, and the vacuum in his chest mocked him all the way home and all through the night.

Chapter Ten

Josie stormed off in search of Luke first thing the next morning. She'd spent a long, sleepless night replaying their conversation in her mind, and she'd finally figured out why he'd departed so abruptly.

Everyone he'd ever cared about had left him in one way or another, and he expected her to do the same. He was withdrawing because he thought she was going to leave.

Just when she'd realized she loved him, he was trying to shut her out.

Well, she wouldn't let him get away with it. Thanks in part to his confidence in her, she'd finally started trusting her heart, and her heart told her to track him down and set things straight.

She found a note taped to his front door saying he'd gone to Kansas to inspect a horse and wouldn't be back until Monday morning. Adding insult to injury, the note was addressed to Manuel instead of her.

She stopped by the Perez house on the far side of the ranch to give Manuel the message. It was Consuela's day off, and Josie found her preparing a big Sunday breakfast for Manuel. "Strikes me as mighty odd that he didn't mention these plans last night," she huffed to the older woman.

Consuela looked up from the pan of grits she was stirring on the stove. "Did you two have a love-your-squirrel?"

"A what?"

"A love-your-squirrel. You know—a fight."

Even Consuela's comically mangled English couldn't make Josie muster a smile this morning. "You mean lovers' quarrel. And no, we didn't have one." She heaved a sigh. "I wish it were that simple."

With a quarrel, at least they'd have a topic out in the open, something concrete to discuss and resolve. Instead, she was grappling with the ghosts of Luke's past. Luke had misinterpreted her remarks because he expected her to leave. In his mind, involvement equaled abandonment. He was avoiding her to avoid getting hurt.

She should be flattered, she told herself; the fact he'd gone to such lengths to stay away from her indicated how much he cared. But it also indicated how unwilling he was to trust her, and the realization left her hurt and angry and frustrated.

She tried to overcome it by spending the rest of the weekend in optimistic action. She worked feverishly on the quilt, hoping with each stitch that Luke could learn to trust her as he'd helped her learn to trust herself.

He continued to avoid her on Monday. He didn't return the messages she left on his answering machine, he stayed away from the lodge, and he completely altered his routine, making it impossible for her to catch up with him.

Josie's irritation grew with each passing hour. When he failed to show up for a meeting to review layouts for the new advertising campaign, her temper blew a fuse.

It was one thing to avoid her personally, and quite another to prevent her from doing her job. With profuse apologies to the ad agency's account executive who'd driven all the way from Tulsa for the meeting, Josie yanked on her jacket and stalked out of the lodge. She'd find Luke if it took all day, and she'd get things settled if it took all night.

She finally located him in the stables, taking inventory of the tack. He looked up as she approached, and his eyes took on a shuttered, wary look that nearly broke her heart.

Darn him, she thought channeling her pain into anger. He didn't even want to give her a chance.

She jammed her hands in her pockets to hide the fact that they were shaking. "Care to tell me what's going on?"

"What do you mean?"

"You know darn good and well what I mean." She managed a tight smile. "But on the one in ten million chance that you don't, let's start with why you didn't show up for the ad agency meeting this afternoon."

Luke picked up another set of reins and turned them in his hands, examining the leather for signs of wear. "Maybe I forgot."

Right. And maybe aliens airlifted you to Mars for a quick game of ticktacktoe. Josie bit back the sarcastic retort, forcing herself to sound calmer than she felt. "So what's the explanation for your disappearing act the other night?"

Luke shrugged. "We agreed to keep our relationship professional. Things seemed to be getting out of hand, so I left. No big deal."

No big deal? Was he really so callous he didn't know how she felt? Did he really feel nothing himself? She swallowed back a sense of outrage along with a painful lump in her throat.

It was a big deal, all right—as big a deal to him as it

was to her. He wouldn't have gone to such pains to stay away from her if it weren't.

All the same, it was hard to rebut the logic of his words or the offhanded, impersonal tone of his voice. Her confidence wavered. Could she be wrong? Was it possible he didn't share her feelings? Maybe she was nothing more than a small, insignificant part of his life—just one of many women he might be attracted to, one who also happened to be an employee.

She rejected the thought as soon as it formed. *No.* Regardless of how casually he acted, she knew his feelings for her weren't casual at all. She'd started to trust her heart in the past few weeks, to have faith in her own judgment, and she wouldn't stop now. Both her heart and her head told her he was bluffing.

Well, two could play at this game, she thought determinedly. She forced what she hoped was a collected expression on her face. "I see. Well, since you're so dedicated to professionalism, I'm sure you'll want to look at the ad layouts as soon as possible."

Luke looped the rein over a hook on the wall and pulled off another. "I changed my mind. I don't want to advertise the lodge."

Josie felt like the bottom had just dropped out of her heart. All pretense of composure dropped with it. "You can't be serious."

"I can. And am."

"But why?"

He avoided her eyes. "I just don't want to do it."

"You don't want the lodge to be profitable?" she pressed.

He lifted a shoulder. "Cattle prices are picking up. This time next year the ranch might be doing well enough to shut the lodge down. I don't want it all booked up with a bunch of tourists."

Josie stared at him, stunned. "You're going to close the lodge?"

His hands jerked over the leather, his voice terse. "I've made no secret of how I feel about it."

"But that was before you knew why your father built it!" Didn't the knowledge that his father had loved him count for anything? She'd thought it had. He'd opened up, stopped isolating himself. He'd become more accessible. She'd thought his feelings of rejection had eased, along with his resentment of the lodge.

Luke shrugged again and turned back to studying the tack. "It's my ranch, and I'll do as I damn well please."

Hurt and anger roiled through Josie. He wasn't even bothering to break it to her gently. He evidently didn't care about all of the hard work she'd put into the lodge—all the late nights and early mornings and weekends, all of the plans and programs and projections.

He evidently didn't care about her feelings.

He evidently didn't care about *her*.

She was grateful for the anger pulsing through her veins, because it gave her the strength to do what she had to do.

She stepped in front of him, forcing him to look at her. "You can do as you damn well please, all right, but you'll do it alone. If you don't want the lodge to succeed, it's your business. But I won't stay around and watch it fail."

A flicker of something—pain...relief...both?—flashed through his eyes before the carefully guarded expression returned. "I didn't expect that you would."

Josie froze. *So that was it.* With icy clarity, she saw what he was doing. He was trying to drive her off. If he made her go now, she couldn't leave him later.

Pain ripped through her like buckshot. She'd wondered

if he could love her back; well, here was her answer, she thought bitterly. *No.* Not because he didn't, not because he couldn't, but because he simply wouldn't.

He wouldn't allow himself to. He was too afraid of being shut out, left alone or abandoned. The only proof she'd ever get that he loved her was that he was driving her away.

She stared at him, her heart aching. She wanted to reach out to him, to help him, to somehow save him from his self-imposed sentence of loneliness. But deep in her soul she knew there was nothing she could do, nothing she could say that would make him trust her. And without trust, love didn't have a chance.

He shifted the reins to his other hand. "You don't have to worry about your job reference. I'll make sure you get a good one." His eyes remained riveted on the leather in his hand. "And I won't hold you to our agreement. You don't have to stay till February."

She swallowed hard, struggling to keep the tears at bay, to retain some shred of dignity. "Good. Because I don't want to stay where I'm not wanted." She averted her face, but tears were already streaking down her cheeks. She didn't want him to see her cry. She'd given him her heart; all she had left was her pride.

"I'll go and pack my things." If she hurried, she could be on her way by dark.

"Consuela." Luke opened the door wider, surprised to find the housekeeper standing on his front porch. The woman had been coming and going by the side door for as long as he could remember. "Since when did you start knocking?"

Consuela shook the rain off her umbrella and propped it beside the door, clutching a bulky plastic bag against her black raincoat. "Since you started acting like a stranger."

Luke's hand tensed on the brass doorknob. "What do you mean?"

"The Luke I know has more sense than to chase off the best thing to come to this ranch since his own mother."

Lightning streaked across the late-afternoon sky, and a gust of water blew onto the wide, covered porch. Luke scowled. Ever since the confrontation with Josie, he'd felt lower than a snail's belly. He was in no mood for company, much less a lecture, but he couldn't send Consuela away in this storm.

"Come in before you drown, Consuela."

She handed him the bag as she stepped inside. Luke set it on a side table and helped her out of her coat. "For your information, I didn't chase her away. She quit."

Consuela narrowed her eyes. "You're rude and obnoxious, you won't let her do her job, you tell her you want to close the lodge. I call that chasing her off."

Luke shrugged. "She wouldn't have been here in a few months, anyway."

"Not now, she won't." Consuela snatched her coat away from Luke, picked up the bag and marched down the long hall toward the kitchen.

With a sigh Luke followed her. "She's been offered a job at a big new hotel in Tulsa. We can't compete with that. The novelty of working on a ranch would have worn off by the time our agreement was over, anyway. She'd have gotten tired of being stuck out here in the middle of nowhere. Besides, by the first of the year, she probably would have decided we were nothing but a bunch of country hicks and hayseeds."

"Sounds like you're describing Cheryl, not Josie. You under X-rate this girl."

"Estimate. The word is *underestimate*."

Consuela shot him a knowing look as she lifted the teakettle from the stove. Luke ran a hand down his face and watched her fill it with water at the sink. He'd swear she sometimes deliberately mispronounced words just to make him repeat them.

She placed the kettle on a burner and turned toward him. "Josie's not like that ex-wife of yours. She loves this place." She stepped closer and peered up in his face, her eyes sharp and bright as razors. "And she loves you."

Luke's muscles froze, but his insides churned. "Did she say so?"

"She didn't have to. Any fool could see it. And any fool could see you have feelings for her, too."

He didn't try to deny it, just tried to divert her back to the topic of Josie. "If she feels anything for me, it's because she's on the rebound from her called-off marriage."

"Bah!" Consuela shook her head as well as her hands. "There was nothing for her to rebound from. You don't believe that any more than I do."

She was right, he realized. He didn't. He hadn't in weeks. He shoved his hands into his pockets. "Well, there's a big difference between attraction and love."

"Yes," Consuela said, nodding her head sagely. "With attraction, the feeling is all about the person's outsides. With love, you care about what's in here." She laid a plump hand against her ample chest. "Most people know in their hearts when it's real. But some people won't listen to their hearts. They're too scared or stubborn or pea-headed."

"Pigheaded," Luke corrected absently.

Consuela nodded shrewdly.

She'd done it again. "I don't suppose you're talking about anyone we know," he said irritably.

Consuela ignored his sarcasm. "You let that girl go, you'll be making the worst mistake of your life. She loves you, and I can prove it." She cocked her head toward the plastic sack she'd placed on the counter. "Go look in the bag."

Luke didn't know why his heart was pounding like the pistons on his tractor or why his mouth felt like he'd just chewed a piece of chalk. Nothing that could fit in a piece of plastic would convince him that Josie wasn't a heartache waiting to happen.

He lifted the sack gingerly, as if it might explode. Annoyed at himself, he grabbed it with both hands and dumped the contents on the counter.

It looked like half of his old quilt—the front half, without the stuffing. Had Josie or Consuela taken it apart? He stared at it, uncomprehending. "What's this? What's going on?"

"Josie was making you a new quilt. She wanted to surprise you with it at Christmas."

He gazed back at the material in his hands. Now that he looked at it, he could see the fabrics were different, the colors were brighter, the stitching less even than the original.

"She's leaving it behind," Consuela said. "Said she had no use for it now."

Luke continued to stare at it, stunned. "You knew she was making it?"

Consuela nodded. "I helped her take down the one in the lodge so she could copy it."

"But why? Why was she doing this?"

Consuela gave an owlish grin. "Figure it out for yourself, Luke. But you'd better hurry. She was nearly packed when I left."

Luke fingered the half-finished quilt, his mind flashing back to the first time Josie had seen his mother's handiwork. Her words echoed in his mind: *A lot of love went into making that. I bet you could feel it when you wrapped it around you.*

Was Josie wanting to wrap him in her love, too? His heart jumped and contracted like a patient being resuscitated in a coronary ward. This was not an ordinary gift, not the sort of thing an employee usually gave the boss at Christmas or one casual friend gave another. This was personal. This was meaningful. This was a gift from the heart.

He ran a callused finger across the embroidery at the edge, a knot forming in his throat as he recognized Josie's handwriting. "Shoot for the stars." *Your mother wanted you to follow your dreams,* Josie had said.

When had he quit dreaming? About the same time he'd stopped trusting, he realized. He'd stopped looking for shooting stars when he'd ducked his head and crawled into his emotional bunker.

A trace of Josie's perfume drifted up from the quilt. He raised it to his face and inhaled deeply, absorbing a few hard truths along with her soft scent.

For years he'd thought of himself as unlovable. Rejected by his father, deserted by his wife and plagued with guilt over his mother's death, he'd erected walls to keep people from getting close. He'd thought he was protecting himself from getting hurt any further, but his fortress had turned out to be a cage. He'd managed to lock other people out, all right. But he'd ended up locked inside.

Then Josie had come along with her warmth and laughter and understanding, and had knocked holes in all his defenses. Was he going to stay in his self-made prison even though the door was wide open? Or was he going to step outside and build a life with the woman he loved?

The woman he loved. A sense of amazement filled his chest, quickly followed by a sense of purpose.

The woman he loved. That's what Josie was, all right.

And if the quilt in his hands meant what he hoped it meant, she loved him, too. Together they had a chance at the kind of happiness his own parents had known, the kind Consuela and Manuel had together. Without her, he had no chance at all.

Consuela was right. Josie was the best thing that had ever happened to him. He'd be a fool to let her get away just because he feared she might someday leave. She was leaving *now*, for heaven's sake.

He had to stop her. Then he had to do whatever it took to make her stay for the rest of her life.

He gave Consuela a sudden, hard kiss on the cheek. "You're a nosy old busybody, and I love you for it."

Her broad face creased into a smile, her many chins quivering in delight. "Save the sweet talk for Josie," she said.

But Luke was already on his way out the door.

"Dadblast it!" Josie banged her hands on the steering wheel in frustration, accidentally hitting the horn.

Her car was stuck in the mud...again. In her hurry to get away from the ranch, she'd taken the shortcut by the barn, and now she could just kick herself. Why, oh *why* hadn't she remembered what rain did to this road?

Maybe she could get some traction by placing cardboard under the tires. Heaven only knew she had enough of it with her—the interior of her car was stacked with boxes from the floorboards to the roof. She twisted around in the seat and ripped the lids off several of them.

Clutching the box tops, she stared out the windshield and hesitated. It was a downpour, nearly as bad as when she'd first arrived here.

"A little water never hurt anyone," she muttered. She couldn't hurt any worse than she already did, anyway. Besides, she couldn't afford to wait out the storm. The afternoon light was rapidly fading, and she was determined to get away from this place tonight if it killed her.

It was already killing her. Her heart felt like it had been cut from her chest with a pair of pinking shears.

She pulled up the hood of her windbreaker and yanked open the door. Cold, driving rain slashed at her face like icicles, making it nearly impossible to see. Holding on to her car, she groped her way to the back and bent down to place the box tops under the tires. It looked like she'd gotten wet for nothing, she realized with a heavy heart; the cardboard was rapidly disintegrating in the rain. She straightened just as a pair of bright headlights rounded the barn.

Luke's truck. Her heart lurched and sank still farther in her chest. *Great, just great,* she inwardly moaned. The only thing that could make this awful situation worse was another encounter with Luke, and it looked like that was just about to happen.

She watched him climb out and bound toward her, hating the way her mouth went dry at the sight of him. He wore a yellow rain slicker and a cowboy hat, and the rain ran off it in rivulets.

"Josie...thank God I caught up with you. We've got to talk." His voice was rough and urgent, and he spoke loudly to be heard over the rain.

Josie shook her head and tried to turn away. "There's nothing left to say."

"There's a lot to say, but I'd rather say it someplace dry. Come on. We can talk in the barn."

She could tell from the set of his jaw that he wasn't going to give up. Unless she wanted to stand here and shout at him in the downpour, she didn't have any choice. With a nod of resignation, she slogged beside him toward the large building.

The barn was dark and quiet and dry, filled with the rich smell of hay and horses. It reminded her of the first time she'd met him, and the memory wrenched her heart.

Luke unfastened his slicker, pulled a handkerchief out of his pocket and offered it to her.

"Thanks," she mumbled, wiping her rain-streaked face.

"We've got to quit meeting like this," he said with a crooked grin, pulling off his hat.

He was breaking her heart all over again, being so warm and kind and charming. It only reminded her of all the reasons that she loved him and the fact he was incapable of loving her back.

He tossed his hat onto an old bench by the wall and took a step toward her. "Consuela showed me the quilt you were making."

Josie's face burned, and she died a thousand deaths. It was bad enough that she was trapped in a one-sided love affair; now she had to suffer the humiliation of having him know exactly how far gone she actually was. "It was just something to fill my evenings," she mumbled.

"Is that a fact?" He stepped still nearer, his mouth curved in a smile that struck her as downright dangerous. "Well, I've got better ways to fill your evenings than that."

Oh, mercy—she could take anything but this. What was he doing? Taunting her? Mocking her? Deliberately trying to drive her crazy?

He placed his hands on her arms, and his touch made her tremble. She tried to turn away, but he wouldn't let her. "Josie, honey, I've been such a fool. I thought if I didn't let you get close, if I didn't care about you, I wouldn't get hurt when you left. I tried my darnedest to keep my distance from you, but I fell for you like a ton of bricks the first time I saw you. And the more I got to know you, the deeper in love I fell."

Her breath froze in her lungs. She couldn't breathe, she couldn't move. All she could do was stare. "What did you just say?" she finally managed to whisper.

He edged closer, his arms moving to her back. "I said I love you, Josie. And I want to do whatever it takes to make you stay."

Josie gazed at him, her heart in her throat. She knew what it cost him to say this, what a huge step he was taking. She knew how hard it was for him to trust, for him to risk his heart.

It had been just as hard for her to trust her own. But he'd just confirmed that she'd been right to do so—that her judgment was sound and solid, that her heart's compass was true and on target.

Her heart took flight, soaring to the rafters of the barn.

"What can I do to make you stay?" he repeated, his voice a whisper, his eyes searching hers.

"Well…" Josie's grin wobbled a little. "You might try asking me."

The look in Luke's eyes mirrored the way she felt. "If I'm going to ask you a question, I might as well make it one that counts."

"Shoot for the stars, I always say," Josie whispered.

"All right. I will." He abruptly dropped down to one knee on the hay-strewn floor, clasped both her hands and gazed up at her, his heart in his eyes. "I love you, Josie, and I want to spend the rest of my life with you. I want you to have my children, to share my days and nights, to grow old and gray with me. I can't promise you the moon and the stars, but I can promise you we'll aim for them together. Josie, will you marry me?"

She gazed at him, her heart full and overflowing. "Yes. Oh, I love you so, Luke. Yes. Yes. Yes!"

The next thing she knew, he was on his feet and she was in his arms.

Outside, the rain continued to fall. And somewhere above the clouds, a shooting star streaked across the sky.

* * * * *

If you enjoyed
HAVE HONEYMOON, NEED HUSBAND,
be sure to pick up Robin Wells' next novel,
PLAIN JANE GETS HER MAN,
coming November 1997 from Silhouette Romance.

Share in the joy of yuletide romance with brand-new
stories by two of the genre's most beloved writers

DIANA PALMER
and
JOAN JOHNSTON
in

LONE STAR CHRISTMAS

Diana Palmer and Joan Johnston share their favorite
Christmas anecdotes and personal stories in this
special hardbound edition.

Diana Palmer delivers an irresistible spin-off of her
LONG, TALL TEXANS series and Joan Johnston crafts an
unforgettable new chapter to **HAWK'S WAY** in this wonderful
keepsake edition celebrating the holiday season. So
perfect for gift giving, you'll want one for yourself...and
one to give to a special friend!

Available in November at your favorite retail outlet!

Only from

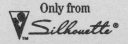

Take 4 bestselling love stories FREE

Plus get a FREE surprise gift!

Special Limited-time Offer

Mail to Silhouette Reader Service™

3010 Walden Avenue
P.O. Box 1867
Buffalo, N.Y. 14240-1867

YES! Please send me 4 free Silhouette Romance™ novels and my free surprise gift. Then send me 6 brand-new novels every month, which I will receive months before they appear in bookstores. Bill me at the low price of $2.67 each plus 25¢ delivery and applicable sales tax, if any.* That's the complete price and a savings of over 10% off the cover prices—quite a bargain! I understand that accepting the books and gift places me under no obligation ever to buy any books. I can always return a shipment and cancel at any time. Even if I never buy another book from Silhouette, the 4 free books and the surprise gift are mine to keep forever.

215 BPA A3UT

Name	(PLEASE PRINT)
Address	Apt. No.
City	State	Zip

This offer is limited to one order per household and not valid to present Silhouette Romance™ subscribers. *Terms and prices are subject to change without notice. Sales tax applicable in N.Y.

USROM-696 ©1990 Harlequin Enterprises Limited

Bestselling author

JOAN JOHNSTON

continues her wildly popular miniseries with an
all-new, longer-length novel

The Virgin Groom

HAWK'S WAY

One minute, Mac Macready was a living legend in
Texas—every kid's idol, every man's envy, every
woman's fantasy. The next, his fiancée dumped him,
his career was hanging in the balance and his future
was looking mighty uncertain. Then there was the
matter of his scandalous secret, which didn't stand a
chance of staying a secret. So would he succumb to
Jewel Whitelaw's shocking proposal—or take cold
showers for the rest of the long, hot summer…?

Available August 1997
wherever Silhouette books are sold.

Silhouette®

Silhouette
™ R O M A N C E ™

COMING NEXT MONTH